BREAK DOWN

Kaily Hart

Copyright © 2017 Kaily Hart

ALL RIGHTS RESERVED. No part of this book may be reproduced or transmitted in any form or by any electronic or mechanical means, including photocopying, recording or by an information storage or retrieval system without the written permission of the author, except where permitted by law.

This is a work of fiction. Names, characters, places and incidents are the product of the author's imagination or are used fictitiously. Any resemblance to actual events, locales, or persons, living or dead, is purely coincidental.

Cover design by The Killion Group, Inc.

DEDICATION

I've always wanted to write military heroes. A guy willing to defend his country? That's hot. But then I got to thinking...what happens after? When former special forces guys are out in the wild? They'd need a special woman who could handle them, right? And so...the Men Out of Uniform series was born. ENJOY!

I also wanted to send a very special thank you to my HartThrobs. You helped me name this book, narrow down options for the cover, name the heroine and you keep me sane. Mostly. Mwah!!

And thank you to Dr. G, my friend the ER doctor. I lived up to my promise of not putting your name in *gasp* a romance book.

And to contractor Mike. You knew your stuff and you were the best. I still think of you often. RIP.

CHAPTER ONE

Roarke gasped, immediately tried to suck in a deep breath. Not his best idea. Instead of a lungful of much needed air, he was engulfed with pain—sharp, intense, piercing. He stilled, waited for the waves of agony to pass, but the throbbing only increased, radiating through him with each shallow breath he managed.

Loud noise reverberated inside his head, but it was muffled, as if it came from far away. He frowned, fought to concentrate, but couldn't lock on to any of the sounds. And why were his hands hot? Burning? He tried to clench them into fists. Couldn't make his fingers work.

He shook his head at the scent of dirt and oil that swamped him. The familiarity of it tugged at him, but he couldn't focus, couldn't pin it down.

He opened his eyes a slit. Blinding light and muted shapes he couldn't quite zero in on jumped out at him. He heard voices, shouts, a loud ringing. Rough hands grabbed at him. He tried to shove them off, but every move he made had pain lancing through him, the intensity of it enough to make his stomach heave and every nerve ending in his body scream in agony. It felt as if his body was being ripped apart, cell by fucking cell.

Had he taken fire? Been hit?

Adrenaline pumped through him, his heartbeat hammering a roar in his ears. He needed to move, take cover, get to safety. He reached out, tried to get leverage on something, anything, so that he wasn't a sitting duck, but nothing seemed to work. He couldn't see, couldn't fucking hear properly.

And then he remembered. Not an IED. Not an enemy pinpointing his location and trying to blow him the fuck up. Not another sniper getting the jump on him. Not an ambush.

His Goddamn hero complex. He'd dived in front of the car of his own accord. It'd been a calculated move. One where he'd accepted the risk of death, just as he had countless times before.

A bitter taste exploded in his mouth and he felt himself falling, even though he wasn't moving. He tried to reach out, grab on to something solid, but his hand met air and pain sliced through his body again. A black shimmering wall of drums rolled across him, oppressive, oily and dark, weighing him down, taking him back to that place, that fucking place he hated, dreaded. It was a place of nothingness where he was helpless, alone and vulnerable.

Aw, fuck.

He swore he'd never allow himself to go back to that place again. Not ever again. He'd decided death was preferable to being dragged back into that hole, but if he was going to go, it wasn't going to be without a fight.

He struggled, with every ounce of strength he had, with everything in him, until he couldn't. And then blackness again, this time…maybe forever…

* * * * *

"Holy crap, did you see the patient in bed ten?"

Marina glanced up at Sarah as she slipped in next to her at the nurses' station.

"The hip dislocation?" she asked, turning back to the monitor.

When there was no response, Marina looked up. Sarah waited. Hand on hip, one eyebrow raised.

Marina laughed. "Yeah, I saw him."

Saw him, was monitoring his vitals and pretty much trying not to gape each time. To say he wasn't exactly representative of her normal patients was the understatement of the day. Maybe the century.

"The guy is seriously ripped," Sarah gushed. "You ever see arms like that before? In the flesh?"

She wished. "Nope."

"Yeah, me either. Do you think he's a gangbanger?"

Marina rolled her eyes.

"I saw this documentary on TV. It—"

"Maybe he just works out a lot," Marina cut in.

"And all those tattoos? The scars?"

Yeah, she'd noticed. Everything. A guy with that many scars had probably spent a considerable time in hospitals.

"Sarah—"

"Okay, okay. Fine."

Marina had already warned her more than once

against gossiping about patients.

"Come out with us after work tonight. A bunch of us are going to hit that fancy new place for overpriced martinis."

Marina sighed. "Can't. I have to get home."

"Just for a little while. A couple of cuties are coming from Radiology."

As if that could sway her. Marina wasn't interested in the cuties. For one, they all looked as if they were about fifteen. Acted like it too.

"I can't."

"Come on, Marina—"

"I really have to get home. Stuart canceled."

Again.

Leaving your active kid on the weekend with an elderly woman who didn't like loud noises was more guilt than Marina could stand sometimes. Unfortunately, she couldn't argue with free babysitting. Or a deadbeat ex-husband.

"What a turd," Sarah sneered.

Yeah. She'd thought when he'd married again, had another child, he might change, grow some balls, step up as a father. What a joke.

Sarah sighed and leaned into her, dropped her voice. "It's going to grow over, you know."

"What is?"

"You know." She motioned to Marina's crotch area.

"Jeez, Sarah." She looked around to make sure no one could hear them.

"Well, it will, although I'm sure the new Doc could help you with that."

"Dr. Howard?" Marina frowned.

"Yeah, he was just checking out your ass. Big

time."

Marina glanced around, but he was nowhere to be seen. "When?"

Sarah rolled her eyes. "You're so clueless. When I came over. He was taking a real good look."

"Right," she scoffed. As if her ass was anything to look at, especially in the loose scrubs.

The last thing she wanted was to get involved with another doctor. Not to date, to sleep with, not to do anything with. No way, no how. Stuart had cured her of that. That's if she were looking. Which she wasn't. She was officially off dating and intended to stay that way. For good.

"He asked you out again, didn't he?"

And it'd been just as awkward as the first time.

"What are you? His personal matchmaker?"

"Hello! He's cute. Young. I heard he's packing and has stamina with a capital 'S'. I wouldn't pass up a guy who's built and can go at it for hours. Just sayin'. I think you're crazy, but whatev."

Sarah gave her a wave, moved off to check on her own patients and Marina let out a long sigh. She'd heard the new doctor was making his way through the single nurses. No thanks. Although…built and can go at it for hours? Damn.

Marina glanced at the clock and made her way across the hall. She had her own patients to check, starting with the guy in ten.

He was still out of it, his big body dwarfing the hospital bed. It'd taken four orderlies just to transfer him onto it when they'd brought him out of the OR. Even prone and covered, he radiated an almost violent, barely leashed power.

His chest, shoulders and upper arms were thick

with muscle and covered in swirling, dark tattoos. Even sedated, he had deep grooves beside his mouth and a slight sneer to his upper lip.

She'd always thought a beard kind of scruffy, but his wasn't very long. His dark stubble was clipped short and low along his jaw and across his upper lip.

She'd noticed the scars the first time she'd taken his vitals. Cuts or stab wounds, each a couple inches long—along with several surgical scars—were scattered across his chest and abdomen. Some were raised and puckered, some flat and faded. He had others as well. On his side, his arms, shoulders.

He looked big and bad, mean and...dark somehow, the only softness a very full lower lip.

"So, Roarke Daniels," she murmured as she began checking his blood pressure. "What's your story, huh?"

She jumped and her heartbeat exploded in her chest when his eyes shot wide open, no hesitation, no gradual awareness. One second he was out, the next fully alert.

"Easy," she gasped.

He went to sit up, sucking in a breath and grabbing his side. He groaned, flung out an arm, hit the rails at the side of the bed and clipped the mobile vitals cart. Marina caught it before it went flying across the room.

"Careful," she warned. "It's okay. Just lie back."

He ignored her, tried to sit up again. His movements yanked at the IV tubing and she steadied the stand before the whole thing got dislodged.

A tough guy like him called for tough measures.

"Roarke," she commanded.

He stilled and his dark gaze snapped to hers. She

leaned down and looked him in the face, eye to eye, so close she could see every single one of his thick, dark lashes. "Lie. The fuck. Back. Down."

His eyes went wide. Yeah, that got his attention. And they were blue. His eyes. They'd looked almost black at first, but were actually a deep, dark blue.

He looked at her for several seconds and then relaxed back against the bed, if you could call it that. The motion had been slow and deliberate, every muscle in his body strained, taut, as if he was anticipating having to move any minute. Or fight.

She placed her hand over the back of his. Even though she kept her touch light, he flinched at the contact. "You're safe here. Okay?"

Who knew what a guy who looked like him could be afraid of? It'd have to be pretty scary.

"I'm Marina. I'll be your nurse."

His gaze met hers again. Wild and unfettered. Strength tinged with desperation and a piercing intensity she wasn't used to in patients coming out of sedation.

Marina automatically began checking the IV connections to make sure nothing had come loose. One hand still cradled his side, his mouth drawn in tight lines, his breathing shallow.

"I can give you something for the pain," she offered.

"No," he ground out, his voice deep, hoarse.

She frowned. Most people were more than happy to take painkillers when they were in pain.

"What happened?" he bit out.

"I heard you tried to stop a car with your body."

His glance took in the room and the equipment in an instant and he eased farther back against the pillows.

"Do you remember what happened?"

"Yeah. Damage?" he bit out.

She assumed he meant him. She glanced up at the clock on the wall after being sure all the connections were still in place. "The doctor will be in—"

"No." When she turned back to him, those dark eyes bore directly into hers. "You. Tell me now or I'll get up and find out for myself."

She'd already seen him move each hand, arm, his legs and feet under the covers, taking his own inventory. Cautioning him about moving was going to fall on deaf ears, so she kept silent.

Marina rolled the computer back over so that she could update his history. "You were very lucky. You—"

"Lucky?" he forced out. "Why do you fucking people always say that?"

You people?

"If you mean medical professionals, perhaps it's because we get to see so many who aren't. You know, who don't make it, that is."

He didn't say anything else, just kept looking at her, one dark eyebrow raised.

Underneath the arrogant assumption she'd do what he asked without question, Marina could see the uncertainty, maybe even a touch of fear. If not for that, she would've insisted he wait for the doctor.

"You sustained a dislocated left hip and were sedated at the scene for transport. A reduction has already been performed."

He frowned. "A what?"

"It was put back in. There didn't appear to be any loose tissue or bone fragments. No complications are anticipated. Alignment looks normal. It was a straightforward procedure. You need to be non-weight-bearing for a week at least. You also have several fractured ribs, also along the left side, some scrapes and bruises and you may experience concussive symptoms, such as headache or nausea. You turned somehow so that the car didn't impact your lower body, which is what usually happens in accidents of this nature."

"It wasn't exactly an accident," he rasped.

Right. Witness reports said he'd come out of nowhere, snatching the boy up and out of the way of the car before taking the full force of the impact.

"You didn't ask about the child," she murmured, when he didn't say anything else.

He closed his eyes. "No."

"Would you like to know that he's—"

"No. I know he's fine."

As far as Marina knew, he'd been disorientated at the scene and in tremendous pain. They'd sedated him as soon as they'd assessed the probable hip dislocation.

She frowned. "How do you know that?"

His gaze met hers again. Dark and focused and piercing, despite the pain he must be in. "Because I made damn sure of it."

Aw, *fuck*.

Roarke took several shallow breaths through his mouth, tried to even his breathing to lessen the impact to his side. He couldn't take a deep breath and he swallowed back the frustration. His side was on fire, his head was pounding, his leg throbbed and if he was honest, he fucking hurt pretty much all over.

He'd leaped and turned his body so that he'd take the full brunt of the hit if he'd calculated wrong. At least, that'd been the plan. He'd taken a risk, made in a split second, something he'd been used to doing every day once upon a time. A risk he'd figured he could end up dead from. The pain told him he'd had no such luck.

Every hospital he'd ever been in smelled exactly the same and it was a smell he'd come to loathe. It burned in his nostrils, the back of his throat, his eyes.

He'd known there was a good chance he'd end up here, maybe it'd been a given the moment he'd started to move.

He'd caught a whiff of her when she'd been close, the nurse, Marina—fresh, sweet—but it hadn't been enough to wipe out the scent of antiseptic that seemed to have seeped into his skin, his bones.

Pain shot up his leg when he tried to move it. His hip was iced, his leg sitting at a weird angle. He'd keep it there. For now.

He rubbed his hand down over his jaw, noticed the scrape on his palm. God, he didn't have time for this shit.

"I need to get out of here," he bit out.

He was already two weeks behind on his flip thanks to unexpected plumbing and electrical issues. The city had taken their sweet-ass time with their inspections and approvals and he'd finally been given the go-ahead. Now this.

"You've been admitted. The doctor wanted you to stay overnight for observation."

Fucking great. He played around with the idea of just getting up and walking out, although the walking thing could be an issue.

Dammit.

"That's it?"

"Barring no complications."

Christ, he wasn't in his twenties anymore. He might keep himself in shape, but his body wasn't honed to be the living weapon it once was. Of course, that was a lifetime so far away it could have happened to someone else. And most of the time he wished it had.

Yeah, he was way too old for the shit he'd pulled. He hadn't moved quite fast enough, hadn't leaped high enough, hadn't twisted his body at the exact moment he'd needed, not at the right angle to avoid the impact to his side.

He'd known it. In the split second he'd committed to his actions he'd known—it was probably all going to go to hell.

He opened his eyes again. She was still here, looking at him in that calm way that pissed him off for some reason. He'd felt something when their eyes met. Shock, heat and something else he couldn't name. He wasn't used to having a reaction like that to anyone, wasn't used to having *any* kind of reaction. Maybe it was the f-bomb she'd dropped.

Man, his throat felt like sandpaper. They'd pumped him full of some crap to put him out and it was an effort to keep the rage under control. And his fucking eyes open. He'd sworn they wouldn't do that to him again.

"Water?" he croaked instead, tried to use his arms to sit up farther, cursing to himself when they shook at the effort.

"Hey, big guy, take it easy."

Roarke froze at the soft, warm hand she'd placed against his chest. The contact was light and fleeting, yet his skin burned at the contact.

He wasn't used to being touched, couldn't remember the last time someone had placed their hand on him. And a woman? Not unless she had a gold-plated invitation and they were going to fuck. Even then there were limits.

"How do you feel?" she murmured.

He choked back a snort. How fucking ironic was that, because he didn't feel, not anymore.

He took a few sips of the cool water she handed him. "Clothes?"

"They were cut off when you came in as a trauma. I was just about to get you a gown."

Damn, they'd been his favorite work pants. He closed his eyes and tried to breathe through the throbbing in his side. Whatever they'd pumped into him was still making him tired.

"How's your pain level?"

God, how many times had he been asked that question? Weeks of it, over and over, until he was sick of it.

"On a scale of one to ten? Yeah, a fucking fifteen."

"The ribs are probably giving you the most pain. There's not a great deal we can do other than—"

"Yeah," he bit out. "I know the drill."

Wouldn't be the first time he'd had busted ribs, although he hoped it was the last. He'd forgotten they hurt like a mother fucker. It was going to make riding his...

Aw, shit.

His bike. No doubt it was still parked where he'd

left it before he'd decided to be a fucking hero.

"My phone?" he choked out. "I need to call someone."

She passed him a bag out from under the bed. "These are what you came in with. I'll be right back."

Roarke watched her walk out, ponytail swinging, and couldn't drag his eyes away. She had a nice body, more than nice, even under the loose scrubs. He might be banged up, but he could still appreciate the sway of her hips, the curves of her ass. And her voice—soft, a little husky, even when she'd sworn at him—appealed to him on some level he had no clue about.

He jerked open the bag. Wallet. Keys. Watch. And phone with a busted screen. This day just kept getting better and better.

He ground his back teeth together. The twins were out of town and he didn't want to bother his crew on the weekend. That left one option, one less than ideal option. He'd just have to man up. He hit dial.

"What's up?"

"Evans." Even the voice through the phone was smug. He could count on one hand the number of times he'd called Jake. "I need a favor."

Roarke cursed at the silence. "Evans?"

"Just wondering what the fuck must be up for you to ask *me* for a favor."

"Yeah, not my first choice, but I need someone to go get my bike."

"Your bike?"

"Yeah, it's outside Marcella's. The sandwich place."

"I know it. Why don't you get it?"

"I'm kind of…tied up right now."

"Cut the bullshit."

He sighed. "I'm in the fucking hospital, okay?"

"Hospital? What happened?"

Roarke closed his eyes. "I just need you to get my bike."

"No chance. Not until you tell me what the fuck happened."

Yeah, Roarke had known exactly how this was going to go down and it was just as painful as he imagined. "I got hit by a car. Superficial injuries."

Jake cursed. "Such as?"

"Some busted ribs."

"And?"

"Evans—"

"*And?*"

"A dislocated hip."

"Jesus, Roarke. What else?"

He glanced down at his arm, noticed the bandage for the first time. "They're the highlights."

Jake was silent for a second, two. "You should know I'm here with Raine, man."

Roarke cursed under his breath. "She doesn't need to know," he muttered.

Jake choked out a laugh. "You never learn, do you?"

"So I've been told. Mostly by you. Tell her I'm fine. I'm great. I'll be home tomorrow. Just…get my bike for me. There's a spare set of keys at Raine's."

He hung up before Jake could say anything else and hoped like hell that was the end of it. He leaned his head back and let his eyes drift closed. Just for a minute.

CHAPTER TWO

Marina sucked in a breath when hard fingers clenched around her wrist.

"How fucking dare you?"

She flinched at the savage intensity of his voice, the violent rage in his eyes. She still held the syringe and tried to tug her hand away, but it was useless. His hold didn't budge.

She frowned. "You were in pain. It's—"

"There are worse things than pain." His dark gaze bore into hers. "Being helpless and out of it are one of them. I can't be that. Got it?"

"It's pain medication. That's all. I swear."

"Do you understand?" he rasped.

She swallowed at everything she saw in his eyes. Pain was a given, but there was a plea there too. Maybe even a hint of desperation. She didn't think this man was used to making a plea to anyone for anything.

She nodded and he released her.

His hold had been unbreakable, but carefully

controlled. He hadn't hurt her, not even a little bit, but she couldn't fight the urge to rub her wrist all the same.

His gaze flicked down to her movements. "Sorry."

The word was low and rough. She'd bet he wasn't used to apologizing either.

"You don't inject anything in that again," he ground out. "Nothing I don't approve first. Got it?"

"Agreed." She gave him a quick nod and leaned in close, because damn it, he wouldn't intimidate her. She poked a finger in his direction. "But if you ever grab me like that again? I'll be forced to throat punch you, injured or not."

His gaze locked on to hers, searing, searching. He wasn't just looking at her. He was seeing her and her throat went dry at the intensity of his eyes. The deep blue was made up of different shades, shifting with the light, framed by long, thick lashes. And God, those eyebrows. Honestly? They were better shaped than hers were.

His mouth lifted at one corner. The move was so slow, so slight, she would have missed it if she hadn't been right up in his face.

His gaze dropped to her mouth for a fraction of a second before returning to hers. Her breath caught, held, but it'd been so quick she wondered if she'd imagined it.

"Yeah," he breathed. "Fair enough."

Marina straightened. Jeez, how could he have smelled so good? Warm and musky and woodsy and…male. So that's what hot-as-hell guys smelled like, even banged-up ones.

She cleared her throat. "I—I need to check your leg placement and the pillow support."

It was best to just get back to business as usual, right? She went to turn the covers back, but his hand clenched in the folds, stopping her.

"I don't have any Goddamn pants on."

"So?" Marina pushed back images of things she shouldn't be thinking about. "I'm a nurse. Do you know how many penises I've seen in my lifetime? How many I've seen today alone? They're all pretty much the same."

Who was she kidding with that one, but she was a professional, Goddamn it.

His grip held firm when she tried another tug.

"Yeah, well, you haven't seen mine," he rasped.

"You're shy? It's—"

"Do I look like a guy who's shy?"

No. He looked like a guy who owned every situation and scenario he found himself in and hated the thought of being out of control at this one. And that's what this was about. Control. But not on her watch.

"Don't be such a baby."

She yanked and pulled the covers aside.

Holy mother of... He was hard and thick and God...*huge*.

"Oh," she gasped.

"Yeah," he drawled. "Still wanna play nurse?"

Marina felt the heat in her cheeks. Crap. That hadn't happened since she was in training. She'd had her fair share of patients who thought they could hit on her. Embarrass her. Be a jackass. Always she'd shrugged it off. No big deal. But this?

If she didn't know better she'd say there'd been a gleam in his eye, almost a full lift at the corner of his mouth, but that had to be her imagination. Because she doubted Mr. Surly knew how to smile.

"Well—" Marina fought for the composure that made her a damn good nurse, although today? It was nowhere to be found. "You know, that's not really that unusual."

Well, *that* right there was, but not the fact that he had an erection.

She swept the edge of the covers back over him. "And the—the pillow placement looks fine."

Everything looked…fine. And he wasn't kidding. He really didn't have anything to be shy about.

She straightened, wondered like hell where to look, what to say, what to do with her hands, but she was saved when the woman rushed into the room.

"*Roarke*."

Roarke closed his eyes. "Christ, this is all I need," he muttered, too low for the other woman to hear.

His girlfriend? Marina thought so until she noticed the man at her side. Wow. Double wow. They made a stunning couple.

Hot attracted hot. It was a known fact. This guy was dressed in a dark suit, the white shirt open at the neck. She might have dismissed him as nice eye candy and nothing else, except for the air of confidence and command that surrounded him. The way he held the woman's hand, the way he looked at her, stood by her, made her stomach clench and her heart ache. And she just knew. He might have been hot, but he was worthy.

"What is this?" Roarke bit out. "A fucking intervention?"

"Roarke, what happened?" the woman demanded.

Roarke looked to the man at her side as if he could do something. He just raised an eyebrow, shrugged and smirked at Roarke.

"Raine." Roarke sighed. "I'm fine. Okay? I'm fine."

Marina slipped out of the room to give them some privacy, but the woman followed her.

"How's he doing?" she asked. "Really?"

"Ah…"

"Please. I'm his sister, his closest relative." She glanced back toward the room. "I'm not sure I can rely on him to tell me the truth."

Marina hadn't seen any resemblance, but there was something familiar in the arch of her eyebrows, the slant of her eyes. And her concern was almost tangible.

"Physically, he's doing very well. He's expected to make a full recovery. The timely treatment of the hip will play a significant role in reducing later complications. He's incredibly strong and resilient, but…"

"But?"

"I've been…a little concerned about him."

Raine frowned. "Oh?"

"Since he regained consciousness, he's been—"

"Oh, God, he was unconscious?"

Raine put her hand up to her chest, her eyes widened.

"He was sedated at the scene and then for the reduction procedure to put his hip back in."

Raine bit her lip and glanced back toward the room again. "He would have hated that."

Yeah, although hate was probably too tame a word.

"Since then, he's been extremely confrontational, almost hostile. He's been uncooperative and—"

She broke off when Raine sighed, smiled a rueful half smile.

Marina frowned. "What?"

"Then he's back to normal. That's how he is."

"Always?"

"These days?" Raine's smile dimmed. "Yeah."

* * * * *

Roarke frowned. "A what?"

This was the first time she'd come back into his room since Raine and Jake had left and she still hadn't looked him in the eyes, not that he blamed her. He didn't care how many other dicks or hard-ons she saw on a regular basis. He wasn't embarrassed, not really, but he liked to control the where and how he got naked and that wasn't it.

It'd been a long time since he'd had a reaction to a woman like that, fast and intense. Maybe never. And he'd had no hope of being able to control it.

"An intercostal nerve block," she repeated as she typed something into the computer she'd wheeled in. "Essentially, it's an injection of an anesthetic, usually with a steroid, around the intercostal nerves that are located under each rib. It's very effective in the management of pain as a result of rib fractures."

Christ, what kind of freak did it make him that her medical speak got him hot? And hard again? Man, he might really be losing it.

"The doctor would prefer you to be sedated."

He clenched his jaw. The pain meds she'd given him earlier had already started to wear off. They might have eased the pain down to bearable, but he'd hated the feeling of it. He despised anything that affected his concentration, his ability to focus, to be aware of what was going on around him. God, he didn't even take so much as an aspirin these days. He'd be damned if they'd give him anything else.

"No. Absolutely not."

"It's—"

"No. Do it without."

"It's...not preferred."

"Do I look like a guy who gives a fuck about 'not preferred'?"

She looked at him then and he frowned, because he couldn't blame the jolt to his stomach on the drugs this time.

What the hell was it about her? He found most people annoying as fuck. They didn't interest him. They didn't amuse him, didn't intrigue him. And women? He'd even given up on the idea of casual sex, had resigned himself to celibacy because the effort just didn't seem worth the return. Even for no-name, one-night-stand sex. He'd realized a long time ago he wasn't built for that anyway.

"Sorry," he ground out, because she gave him that look, the one that said he could do better, the one that made him want to. For her. And just how fucked up was that?

"I just—I can't be put under, okay? I don't care how much it hurts. I just can't be out of it."

"It is possible to do under local, but it can be painful and certainly uncomfortable. I'll talk to the doctor, okay?"

She looked back down at her screen and everything in him froze when she licked her upper lip.

Christ.

Roarke closed his eyes to cut off the visual

stimulation. He didn't even like kissing, so why the hell did he have an overwhelming desire to taste her, to feel that tongue on his, to dominate her with his own?

He cleared his throat. "Will you be there for it?"

He wished he could take back the words as soon as he said them. He'd sounded weak, needy, and he hadn't needed anyone in longer than he could remember.

"I will."

With his eyes still closed, the husky softness of her voice rumbled through him. It might have soothed his shot nerves, but it didn't do a fucking thing for his hard-on.

* * * * *

Roarke groaned as he rolled over onto his good side and lifted his arms up over his head, as instructed. He tried to breathe through the pain but the busted ribs made it pretty much impossible. He hoped like fuck the procedure did something because it was going to be damn hard to do what he needed to do at the house. His crew couldn't take up any more slack.

He closed his eyes as they prepped, wiping him down with something cold and wet. He caught the scent of the antiseptic solution and his stomach churned, twisting his insides. He fought against the rush of memories, the images that played in his head, but knew it was useless. The smell sent him right back to feeling helpless and vulnerable, unable to protect himself, unable to fight. Every. Single. Time.

Roarke reached for his image of a crystal-clear

lake, tuning out the voices of the doctor, the technician, all the other sounds in the room. He let his body sink into place, relaxing every limb, every muscle. He couldn't take a deep breath, so he kept it slow and shallow—in for four seconds, out for four seconds—until his body, his mind, was calm and still.

It was the same technique he'd used to stay immobile for hours at a time while he waited for a target. A human target.

A small hand slipped over his and he flinched from the unfamiliar contact. He couldn't see her from this position, but he knew it was her. Marina. It was probably just his imagination, but he swore he could feel the warmth of her skin, even through the gloves she wore. He had an overwhelming urge to rip them off, to feel the texture of her hand, skin to skin, instead of the smooth, cool surface of the latex.

"Just a few small pinches."

Roarke sucked in a breath as hard fingers probed between his ribs before the small prick. Right. Never believe a fucking doctor when they told you it wouldn't hurt. He waited, counted off the seconds, knowing, hoping it wouldn't be long for the numbness to take over.

Marina stroked his hand—soft, small movements—and he cursed under his breath. He was having a medical procedure where they put a fucking needle under his rib cage and all he could think about was how it'd feel if she stroked him like that, somewhere a hell of a lot harder than his hand.

"Okay, a little pressure."

He clenched his jaw when he felt the needle go under his rib.

Fuck. Me.

Pain he knew. Pain he could handle. Pain he could push through all day, every day. And it didn't really hurt, not on any scale of pain he'd already felt, endured, multiple times. No. It was the sensation, the knowledge, that something pierced him, sliced through skin, muscle, because he'd felt every single one of those stab wounds, sharp and agonizing. It might have been a hell of a lot of years ago, but each one was burned into his memory like a brand.

He still wasn't sorry he'd refused sedation. Anything was preferable to utter helplessness. He couldn't be that. Not ever again.

Her hand shifted in his and he realized he'd turned his own hand into hers, palm to palm, fingers laced tight. There was nothing delicate about her hold. She might have been small, but her grip was solid and strong.

Shit.

He eased back on the clench of his hand, forced his fingers to slide from hers.

He'd been holding hands with his nurse. The one who swore at him. The one who intrigued the hell out of him. The one who'd turned him on—hard and fast—just from a simple look.

His.

Christ. He'd never thought of a woman in terms of *his* anything. Not before Marina anyway.

CHAPTER THREE

Marina walked to the nurses' station and tried to hold back a yawn, hoping like hell the three cups of coffee she'd already downed this morning kicked in soon. It'd rained in the middle of the night and she'd had to use just about every pot and pan she had in her kitchen to catch the leaks. Not to mention the giant bubble of water that had appeared out of nowhere under the paint on the back wall.

She sighed. The roof was just the most recent issue. She'd really stretched herself to buy that house and it was turning out to be the worst decision she'd ever made. After Stuart, of course. She still didn't know how she was going to come up with the eight grand for a new roof.

"How's the hip dislocation?"

She shouldn't have, but she hadn't been able to stop thinking about him. About how his hand had felt wrapped completely around hers, how he'd gripped her, but it hadn't been crushing, as if he'd been careful of his strength, careful of her.

Nancy gave her a dirty look at the question.

"That good, huh?"

"Let's see," Nancy drawled. "He refused all pain meds, took out his own IV and told me he was no longer going to 'piss in a fucking bottle again'."

Nancy grabbed her sweater off the back of the chair and stretched after they'd gone through their hand-over. "I left crutches in there for him. He refused all instruction in how to use them."

She could imagine. "Of course."

"Well, he's all yours, chica," Nancy muttered over her shoulder and gave her a backhanded wave.

It'd been a quiet night and she only had a few patients to look in on. She froze when she got to the doorway of the first room.

He was sitting on the edge of the bed. Someone had brought him clothes because he'd changed into a pair of loose gray sweatpants and a white t-shirt that stretched taut across his chest and around his hard biceps. He sat with his legs spread wide, emphasizing the muscled thickness of his thighs, the bulge between his legs.

She'd seen him shirtless and mostly naked, but somehow the impact of seeing him in regular clothes was so much greater. With the tattoos covering most of his powerful forearms, he looked rough and rugged, hardened in a way that had never appealed to her. Before.

He looked up at her even though she swore she hadn't made a sound. It was with a focus so intense she fought against squirming. He carried a dangerous air around him that should've scared her, but the tingle of awareness she felt every time he looked at her wasn't fear.

She cleared her throat. "I see you made quite an impression on Nancy."

She caught a brief flare of something in his eyes before he masked it. "Who?"

"Your night nurse. How's your side?"

His eyes narrowed. "It hurts."

It was a simple statement of fact. No complaining, no demanding something be done, nothing.

"That's it?"

One shoulder lifted in a slight shrug. "What else is there?"

"I can give you something for the pain."

Dark brows shot down low over his eyes. "No."

"The anesthetic from the block would have worn off, but the steroid should start to take effect soon."

"Yeah." He ran a hand over his side, probing. "I hope so."

"Nancy told me the mother of the boy you saved wants to come in and thank you personally. Maybe bring the boy."

"No." He scowled. "Absolutely not."

She frowned. "Why not?"

He shook his head. "I don't owe that kid or his mother anything. They want to say thank you so they'll feel better by showing their gratitude. To ease the guilt and anxiety and whatever the fuck else they feel. I don't want it and I don't need it. I did what I did because I could. Because I could see what was going down and I have the training and skills to pull it off."

"And what training would that be?"

Because really, who learns how to jump in front of a car? And why?

At first she thought he wasn't going to answer.

"I was Navy," he bit out. "SEAL."

The elite of the elite. Best of the best. She could see it now. And God, it explained so much.

She kept her voice soft. "How long?"

"Long enough."

The words might have been short and harsh, but she felt the emotion that simmered from them all the same. She doubted he'd appreciate the sentiment, but she'd offer it anyway. Because it mattered.

"Thank you for your service."

His gaze zeroed in on hers then, stark and hard.

"I don't want thanks. I don't do anything for thanks. It was nothing. No big deal."

Marina leaned on the side of the doorway and crossed her arms. "Nothing to see here, huh? Wow. That is such bullshit."

"What is?"

"All of it."

One of his eyebrows rose. "Excuse me?"

"You did what you did because you knew you could save that child from serious injury, maybe even death."

He used his arms to ease himself closer to the edge of the bed, wincing with the effort.

"So?" he fired back.

"So, I might even go so far as to say it's ingrained in your nature."

"What is?"

"Bravery. Doing what needs to be done, what's right. Being a hero."

He snorted. "Now who's spewing bullshit? What about me could possibly tell you I'm any type of hero?"

She glanced at his chest. The scars might have

been covered, but she wasn't likely to forget what they looked like.

"I stopped counting at ten," she murmured.

His jaw clenched. A pulse ticked at his temple. "You have no idea how I got them," he ground out.

"No. But you're not going to stand by while someone just repeatedly stabs you. There's a story there."

"Everyone's got a fucking story. I'm no different, no special."

"Yeah, I'm not buying it. You couldn't have known you wouldn't be seriously injured, maybe even killed when you saved that boy. Not for sure."

She'd seen him when he woke up. He'd known he'd saved the child's life. With absolute certainty.

Because I made damn sure of it.

"Know what I think?" she added.

"Not particularly."

"I think you couldn't stop being a hero, even if you wanted to. Even when you try your best to be the biggest asshole you can."

Yeah, his fucking hero complex. It'd gotten him into trouble more times than he could count. It's what had gotten him nineteen fucking stab wounds and six weeks in a hospital, fighting for his life, battling infection after infection. It was why he'd finally quit the Navy. It's why he preferred a nail gun these days to the multitude of weapons he used to carry and knew how to use with deadly precision.

And why the fuck had he told her about being a SEAL? He could have shrugged it off, deflected, hell, flat-out refused to answer. That's what he would have done with anyone else. Why did he feel as if he owed her something? Anything?

Didn't matter. He was out of here and it couldn't come soon enough.

He reached for the crutches leaning against the bed. He was under strict orders not to put any weight on his leg. Man, it was going to be damn hard using them for a week before he got to see the orthopedic specialist. He might not like being told what to do, but he didn't fuck around with recovery. That lesson had been drilled into him and he'd learned. The hard way. He'd follow orders. For now.

Marina motioned to the crutches. "I can give you some tips on—"

"Nah. I got it."

How hard could it be?

He steadied the crutches, gripped the handles and used them to leverage himself off the bed and up in a single move, ignoring the screaming in his side. He tried to balance, position the crutches under his arms, all while keeping his leg off the floor, except the leg of the right crutch slipped and went out from under him. It happened in a fraction of a second, before he could do anything but fall, and he went down—heavy and hard.

Aw, fuck.

The pain was sharp and unforgiving and lashed through him in waves, his stomach churning with it. He glanced up. Marina hadn't moved.

"Are you just going to stand there and watch?" he managed.

"In full stubborn-mule mode I see?"

He snorted. "Christ, what kind of nurse are you?"

"The kind that expects a decent level of respect,

even when you're having a bad day."

A bad day? That would have to be the biggest fucking understatement of the century. He laid his forehead against the cool floor, letting the waves of pain wash over him. He focused on keeping his breathing shallow and steady. The last thing he needed was to pass out. At least he couldn't fall any farther.

When the pulses of nausea finally settled, he lifted his head, braced his arms.

She came over and crouched next to him. He could smell whatever she'd used on her hair, her skin, or maybe it was just her—sweet and fresh. It was almost enough to wipe out the smell of whatever chemical they'd used to clean the floor. Almost.

"Grab the crutches, align them upright, put them together and hold the hand grips in one hand."

It took a second for the calm, even words to register. God, he hadn't even thought about getting back up.

He sighed, wanting to tell her to go to hell, but he did as she said, wincing at the lance of pain in his side as he reached for the crutches.

"Get up on your knees, but don't put any weight on your left knee. Keep it all on the right side."

Right. It sounded so fucking easy.

"Grab the side of the bed with your other hand, anywhere that's comfortable to use as leverage."

He clenched his jaw, could already see how he could make this work.

"Okay, show me those big muscles aren't just for show and pull yourself up. Keep any weight off your left leg."

He narrowed his eyes on hers, gritted his teeth and

used his upper body strength to drag himself up, until he could get his right leg under him. He stood, slow, unsteady, and planted his ass back onto the side of the bed.

He let out a rough breath. His arms might have been shaking, but he'd done it. Yeah, maybe the crutches weren't as easy as they looked.

"Thanks, okay?" he muttered.

She moved to stand in front of him. Sitting as he was, they were almost eye to eye and every muscle in his body stilled.

"I understand needing to be strong and independent, but there's nothing wrong with asking for temporary help from a professional whose job it is to do just that."

"Yeah." He gave a slight nod. "Fair enough."

She gave him a quick smile. "It's why I get paid the big bucks after all."

Christ, did she just wink at him? He let the corner of his mouth lift and wondered if there was a chance his face might crack because he couldn't remember the last time that had happened.

Except with Marina. How could someone be tough as nails but sweet as hell at the same time? And why did that combination turn him the *fuck* on? Big time.

* * * * *

Marina hid a smile as she watched him maneuver on the crutches with a powerful, predatory grace. It'd taken him about five minutes of trial and error before he'd mastered them. Now, he used them with an easy expertise that almost had her jogging just to keep up.

He'd refused the wheelchair ride to the exit. She'd expected nothing else.

She turned to him when they'd cleared the hospital doors and didn't see anyone waiting.

"Your ride not here?"

"Running late."

She pulled out the tiny envelope that had been burning a hole in her pocket all morning. She thrust it at him.

"The mother of the boy you saved asked that you get this. He wrote you a note."

She could almost predict what he was going to say, but she'd promised. He looked at it as if it might bite.

"I already told you," he bit out. "I don't need any thanks."

"Maybe the child—"

"I also don't owe that kid anything."

She sighed, slipped it back into her pocket. "You're a hard-ass, is that it?"

"No. I'm an asshole. Big difference. Known fact. You should probably remind yourself of that. Often."

"And why should I need to do that?"

He moved a step closer to her, forcing her to tilt her head back to look at him.

"Because there's something I've wanted to do since the first time you swore at me."

Marina's throat had gone dry. This close she could feel the heat coming off his big body and her stomach clenched at his nearness.

"And what's that?" she managed.

"Am I discharged?"

The question caught her off-guard. "What?"

"Am I officially discharged from this…place?"

Yeah, she could imagine what he'd been about to

say. She narrowed her eyes on him.

"Am I officially discharged?" he repeated.

"Yes, you signed the papers so—"

"So that means I'm no longer a patient here, right? I'm no longer *your* patient?"

She frowned. "That's right."

"So you don't have any ethical dilemma."

"Any what?"

What the hell was he talking about?

"And you won't get into any kind of trouble?"

"Trouble? For what?"

"This."

Marina gasped when he curved a rough hand around the back of her neck and pulled her into him. She stumbled a step forward, her body slamming hard against his. She reached out to steady herself and ended up with both hands flat against his lean waist. How could a body be so hard, so unyielding?

He hissed in a breath at the contact and her gaze lifted, locked to his. There was heat there—heat and need, dark and sensual.

It was hard to imagine he'd ever been injured. God, he'd been hit by a car yesterday, yet he exuded a confidence and raw vitality she'd never seen in any other man, hurt or not.

She waited, agonizing seconds, while his gaze traced over her face, stopping on her mouth. Her heart slammed against her chest when he lowered his head and molded those full lips to hers. The move had been slow, deliberate. He'd given her plenty of time to move if she'd wanted to, but God, she hadn't wanted to. And then she couldn't.

For a guy so forceful, so aggressive, his lips were soft against hers, almost tender. At first. He licked at her bottom lip before sucking it into his mouth, causing a shaft of heat to explode in her stomach and then lower, between her legs.

She whimpered when he lifted his lips until they barely touched hers. Close, but not close enough.

Marina gulped in air, the blood roaring in her ears, deaf to everything around her. She gasped when his fingers fisted in her hair, sending a tingle of sharp sensation from her scalp through her entire body.

And then his lips were on hers again, his tongue surging into her mouth once, sliding against her own, twice, a third time. The bold, sure movements caused a curl in her stomach she hadn't experienced in a long time, maybe never like this. The flesh between her legs throbbed, ached.

She whimpered when he pulled back again and put a shaking hand to her lips when he straightened. They felt swollen, wet from his. It'd felt as if he were fucking her mouth with his tongue and God…it'd been so long since she'd had a man inside her, on top of her, holding her down.

When she realized his intention, she'd expected hard and forceful. Not hurtful, just more in the take-no-prisoners realm of kissing. He'd kissed her with a patience that had been honed over time and a gentleness she never would have expected.

She took a deep breath in a futile effort to stem the rapid thud of her heart when his hand slid from the back of her neck.

His eyes dropped to her lips for a second before meeting hers. She'd once thought them cold and hard. Now they blazed with an explicit heat that took her breath away.

"Because only an asshole would kiss you when he

has nothing even close to honorable intentions in his head, but he does it anyway."

CHAPTER FOUR

Roarke straightened, stretched, tried to ease out the kinks in his back. It was damn hard nailing window trim while balanced on crutches. It was taking him twice as fucking long to do everything today.

It didn't help that every time he stopped work, the shocked look on Marina's face forced itself into his head. He still couldn't believe he'd kissed her. In anyone's book it'd been a dick move.

That kiss might have been the most selfish thing he'd ever done. It also might have made him the biggest jerk alive, but he hadn't been able to force himself to walk away without a single touch, without a taste of her at least.

He couldn't remember the last time he'd kissed a woman, the last time he'd even wanted to. He'd fucked. A handful of brief, unsatisfying hookups until he'd finally given up on those too. It was fucking pathetic, but one kiss from Marina was so much more than all of those combined. And yet it still hadn't been enough.

She'd kissed him back, there was no question of that, but it'd been soft, tentative. He'd wanted her tongue in his mouth, her hands fisted in his hair, he'd wanted her to grind herself against his hard-on until she came.

What he would have done if she had, he had no clue because he'd had no intention of taking it any further. They'd been standing in front of the fucking hospital for starters.

So they had some insane chemistry or whatever the fuck it was. He could have asked her out. Like a normal guy. Except he wasn't a normal guy. Maybe he didn't even know what that meant anymore.

He'd accepted a long time ago something had been ripped out of him, severed, and he had no clue how to fix it. He still didn't. And maybe he didn't want to. There was safety in being emotionally paralyzed. He'd have to be a moron not to recognize that.

He'd played around with the idea of apologizing. Nixed it just as fast. Anyway, none of that mattered now. He needed to get his head back in the game. He'd had a shitload of work to make up even *before* he'd decided to be a damn hero.

He raised his hands above his head and tried a light stretch of his side, wincing at the twinge. Living in whatever flip had a finished bathroom had always seemed so practical. No commute and he could work all hours of the day and night on his own schedule. And he didn't need much, certainly not all the hassle that came with a fully decked out house, but getting up and down from his mattress on the floor tonight was going to be a bitch. He swallowed against the immediate heat that surged through him because he'd thought about him and Marina on that bed all fucking day. Her soft body under his. At how it might feel to pump into her, hard and deep. How she'd wrap herself around him, maybe dig her nails into his back.

He frowned when he heard the knock. He had people coming and going from the site all the time and not one of them had ever knocked. Besides, he always left the front door wide open.

He put the nail gun aside, snagged the crutches and made fast work to the front of the house. He still had shit everywhere, but he'd spent some of the day reorganizing his equipment and supplies so that he had enough clearance to get around.

He froze when he reached the front door.

"Nice place you have here," she drawled.

"Marina," he breathed. Yeah, to the untrained eye it must look like a disaster zone. "What are you doing here?"

It was the first time he'd seen her in anything other than the blue scrubs. The black stretchy pants emphasized the shape of her legs, the snug white tank the shape of her breasts. Small, curvy and compact. His throat went dry.

Her gaze swept over the big open room with its new drywall. "This is some hardcore renovating. You wouldn't know anything about roofs, would you?"

"Roofs?"

"Yeah, apparently I need a new one."

"Ouch."

She sighed. "Yeah."

There was a lot simmering in that one word. He should mind his own business, stay the hell out of it.

"Where's your house?"

Too late.

She frowned. "Why?"

"Maybe I can take a look?"

At her raised eyebrows, he cursed under his breath. There was nothing he hated more than trying to explain himself. Unless it was talking about himself.

"I'm a general contractor. I'm not just renovating this house. I flip houses for a living. I might know a thing or two about roofs."

"Oh. I'm over on Gibson. It's—"

"The house with the yellow mailbox?"

She frowned. "How did you know that?"

Shit. She was close, practically in his backyard.

"I look at all houses that go on the market within a fifteen-mile radius between a certain price range."

He was always looking for the next house. Plus, he needed to keep a close watch on what houses were selling for. He'd looked at her house himself when it was for sale, discarded it because there'd been too many unknowns.

"You don't need a new roof," he bit out.

"What? Are you sure?"

"Absolutely. The roof on that house was in great condition. You probably have a leak. I have a roofing guy who can come by to take a look at it. Fair warning, though. Mike will arrive in a beat-up old truck. He'll be wearing dirty work clothes. He'll scribble a bunch of stuff in an old notebook. But he's the best roofing guy there is. He's honest and fair. He'll tell you exactly what you need. Or don't need. Okay?"

"Um…sure. Thank you."

He heard the relief, the hope in her words. It shouldn't have mattered to him, but the burn in his chest told him it did.

"So what are you doing here?" he repeated.

His stomach clenched when she pulled the small envelope out of her bag. He ground his back teeth together until his jaw popped. He didn't need her to tell him what it was.

"Didn't we already have this conversation?" he bit out.

And they both knew how that'd ended.

"I don't want thanks, I don't need gratitude and I'm not looking for any fucking accolades," he added.

She kept her arm outstretched, her gaze steady. "I promised I'd give it to you, so I will. Take it. Even if you trash it, burn it, whatever."

He let out a rough breath. "You always keep your promises?"

She frowned. "Always. Don't you?"

"Yeah."

Because she probably didn't realize how rare that was, he reached out and grabbed the envelope, stuffing it in the back pocket of his jeans before he changed his mind.

"How did you find me?"

"I—" Hot color flooded her cheeks. She cleared her throat. "You put this address on your discharge paperwork. I—I couldn't help notice. I only live a few streets over, so I thought…"

"Thought what?"

He was being an ass, because he could see it in her eyes—attraction, interest. Hunger.

All of a sudden all those fantasies he'd tormented himself with all day didn't seem so farfetched after all. And that was a problem. A big problem.

She lifted her chin a fraction. "I want to know why you kissed me."

Fuck.

"Are you here for an apology?"

Because he would. If she wanted him to. She deserved a lot more than that.

"No. Unless you're sorry about it."

Yeah, he couldn't claim that.

"I was thinking…maybe you could do it again. You know, when I'm not caught off guard. Or on duty."

Holy. Shit.

All the air left his lungs. His usually steady heartbeat kicked into high gear. Need burst in his gut and lower until he hardened in an instant.

Kissing wasn't his thing, so why did he have the urge to grab her to him and do just that? Just when he thought it was the dumbest idea he'd ever had, he leaned forward, convincing himself none of it mattered. And that he'd just take a taste. One taste. Because no way could it have been as good as he remembered.

"Wait."

He froze. Was she kidding?

"Last time I wasn't ready." She took a deep breath, licked her lips, rubbed them together.

If need wasn't a pounding, roaring drumbeat inside him he might have smiled.

"Okay." She nodded. "I'm ready."

When he didn't move she frowned. "Or did that just destroy the spontaneity?"

She was close, so close he could smell her hair. He bent toward her and his breath caught when she stepped forward, tipped her mouth up to his.

Balanced as he was with the crutches, he could only use one arm. He slid a hand around to her lower back, eased her the final few inches until she was pressed up against him.

She sucked in a breath. Yeah, no way she could miss the hard-on, but he wanted to be sure she knew what she was dealing with. Full disclosure before he put his hands on her.

He wanted to crush his mouth against hers, take what she offered, take it hard and fast from the get-go. Instead, he leaned down and sucked her bottom lip into his mouth until she gasped. He swept his tongue over it, tugged on it again, was rewarded with another gasp.

Her tongue touched against his, soft and gentle at first, the second time more daring. The third time she whimpered and thrust into his mouth, bold and forceful.

Yeah. Fuck.

He groaned, angled his head and covered her mouth with his, taking over control, sucking at her tongue, sweeping his own against and over hers, dominating it and her.

Her hands fisted in the t-shirt at his waist when he ground her lower body against his. She trembled, arched farther against him. And then her hands were under his shirt, against the skin of his lower back, hot and soft and smooth.

Damn. He wanted his hands on her skin. Now. He pulled back, swallowed the shaft of satisfaction at her moan and edged his fingers up and under her own shirt.

Everything in him stilled when movement behind her caught his attention.

"*Shit.*" He sighed at the familiar truck at the curb. "My guys are here."

Her eyes opened, slow and dazed. "What?"

"My crew. They just pulled up."

"Seriously? *Now?*"

Her lips were red and swollen and wet from his, her eyes glazed with need, her cheeks flushed.

"Yeah."

Perfect fucking timing. Today, of all days, they had to check in here before knocking off.

She stepped back from him, her eyes flicking down to the bulge he had no hope of hiding. She was breathing heavy and damn, her nipples were hard points against her tank. What he wouldn't give to have had a chance to see them, take them in his mouth, suck on them until—

"I get off work tomorrow at the same time." Her voice was low, husky, and it sent a shiver down his spine. "I could swing by here and—"

"Marina," he breathed, running an unsteady hand down over his face because what the fuck was he really doing? "Do you even see me?"

"What do you mean?"

He spread an arm wide.

"Look at me. I'm a loner. A moody asshole. A mean son of a bitch if you like. If you called me antisocial that'd be a huge fucking understatement. The last thing I want or need is a girlfriend."

There. Upfront. Blunt and to the point.

"Good. I'm not interested in being one."

He frowned. "I'm just trying to be honest."

She gave him a long, pointed look. "Try harder."

His lips tightened at the implied criticism, the challenge in her words. What the fuck did that even mean? He didn't get a chance to ask because she turned to go. He couldn't have stopped his eyes dropping to the curves of her ass if his life depended on it.

He gave her more leeway than he would any other person. And just why the hell *was* that?

* * * * *

Marina didn't knock this time. She wandered in the open front door, stepping over and around...stuff. Construction stuff. Everywhere. It was hard to imagine Roarke living in this mess.

He'd taken out some walls, stripped out everything down to its shell. It's what she'd imagined doing to her own house. She'd had a bunch of grand plans to open up the living room, renovate the kitchen, the two bathrooms, build out a room as a playroom for Sam. That was, before the bills piled up and living week-to-week was as much as she could manage.

She ran her hands down each thigh as she wandered through to the kitchen. So she was nervous. So what? It wasn't everyday she decided she was going to go for it with the hot, sexy guy. The hot, sexy guy who didn't want anything permanent. What could be more perfect?

God, she'd never done anything like this before. Not even close. She didn't even have a regular sitter for Sam. Luckily, she'd swallowed the guilt and organized a last-minute sleepover for her, tried to convince herself it didn't make her a bad mommy.

She'd agonized over what to wear. In the end she'd gone with simple—a simple black top and flowy black-and-white, knee-length skirt. Heat flooded her face. Simple and easy to take off might have factored into it. She'd even rummaged for nice underwear she hadn't worn in longer than she could remember. She might have had to dust those off.

"Hey."

Marina jumped when Roarke appeared out of nowhere. He hadn't made a sound, even with the crutches.

Oh boy.

He'd just showered, his hair still damp. He was wearing jeans and another of those snug t-shirts, the ones that hugged his chest, showed off his muscled biceps and hinted at the ink that covered him. It was almost as good as the sight of him with the dusty cargoes and the tool belt yesterday. Almost. His beard was cropped close to his hard jaw as if he'd recently trimmed it. Her stomach starting flip-flopping. Hard.

"Hey yourself."

Even her voice sounded shaky, mirroring the tiny tremors that chased up and down her legs.

Was there some type of etiquette in these situations? Should she do something? Say something? Should he?

"Mike went by to take a look at your roof today."

God, as if she needed the extra jolt to her stomach. "And?"

She swallowed, reminded herself it couldn't be worse than the eight thousand she'd already been quoted.

"The flashing around a pipe and a couple vents needs to be replaced. He said about five hundred. Looked as if it'd been leaking for a while. Maybe a little more if he needs to replace any tiles or plywood once he starts."

"Dollars?" she breathed.

"Yeah."

God. The guy she'd gotten the quote from had arrived in a fancy new truck, had been wearing a button-down shirt and had taken notes on a tablet. He'd emailed her the quote before he left. That should have been her first clue.

"I— That's great. Thank you."

His gaze raked over her and her heartbeat kicked up again.

"Marina, I've been thinking," he ground out. "This was a mistake."

"I—" Marina frowned. "What?"

"I'm sorry. I can't do this."

"This?"

He waved his hand in her general direction. He still hadn't looked her in the eyes.

"Are—are you serious?" she managed. She should have felt embarrassed, awkward, but fuck all that.

"I'm sorry, I—"

"Do you realize I'm wearing my most uncomfortable bra?"

"What? God, *why*?"

"Because it makes my tits look perky. And I shaved my legs for you, damn it." She swallowed back the sting at the back of her throat. "And not just my legs. Not that you'll ever get to see *that*."

Heat flooded her cheeks when his gaze dropped between her thighs.

"Do you know how many dates I've been on? Ever?"

His eyes met hers. Finally. "Marina—"

"None. A big fat zero. And this was going to be a first for me too. Goddamn it, I took a chance on you, Roarke. I stepped out of my comfort zone and took a chance on you and you blew it."

His eyes narrowed on her. "So, you're here for a quickie? Is that it? You're cock hungry and you think I can do something about it?"

If she hadn't gotten to know him so well she'd say his look was detached, even cold, but there was heat in his dark eyes. For her.

So she came to sleep with him. No strings, just hot sex. So what and why not? Why couldn't she just own it? She was a grown woman. With needs. Adult woman needs. And her pussy wanted *him* to satisfy those needs.

She felt hot color flood her cheeks, fought to keep from slapping her hands up to cover them. God, even just thinking a word like that made her blush.

One of his eyebrows lifted. "Must have been a good thought," he drawled.

She lifted her chin. For one, she had to if she wanted to look him square in the eyes. For another, it just might help with projecting the confidence she didn't have when it came to stuff like this. Or not.

"Yes," she managed.

"Yes?" He frowned. "Yes what?"

"Yes, I'm here for a quickie. Not my choice of expression, but yes, technically you could say I'm cock hungry and yes, I absolutely think you can do something about it." She glanced down at his crotch, at the bulge she couldn't miss. That more than anything gave her the courage to continue. "In fact, I know you can."

He closed his eyes for a split second, shook his head. "I'm a coward, Marina."

Was he kidding?

"I know for a fact that's not true. In so many ways."

"Then I'm a coward about stuff like this."

She took a step toward him and frowned when he inched back with the crutches, the move awkward. "Stuff like this?"

He waved a hand in her direction. "Man, woman, dating stuff. I'm not wired for it. Not anymore."

"That's such bullshit."

His brows shot down low over his eyes. "You have no idea what you're dealing with here."

She took another step, wanting, needing to touch him. He eased back out of her reach. Again.

"Why are you moving away from me?" she murmured.

"Because you scare the hell out of me."

She froze at that. "I do? Why?"

"Dammit, Marina. Because you deserve more than a hard fuck and no follow-up and yet that's exactly what I want to give you, that's all I *can* give you."

"Roarke—"

"I won't call you, Marina. Even if we screw and it blows my mind, I still won't call you afterward."

"Why not?"

He looked at her for so long she thought he wasn't going to answer.

"I just won't," he finally ground out. "When I came back…"

"Came back? Came back from where?"

His features hardened.

"Never mind."

She wasn't sure she wanted to know, not really. Who knew what hell he'd seen, experienced? She couldn't hope to imagine, had no context to be able to understand.

"Look." He pushed out a rough breath. "You

deserve so much better than that. I thought I could, but I can't. I'm really sorry. I am."

"God, if you say that one more time I'll—"

"What? Throat punch me?"

Marina smiled—sort of— although it was the last thing she felt like doing.

He ran the fingers of one hand up over his face and into his hair, clenching it in place in the thick strands. The muscles of his biceps bulged.

"Honestly? I've been a loner for so long I don't know how to be anything else."

"Oh, Roarke."

His eyes flashed dark. "I'm not looking for a pity fuck either."

She burst out laughing this time. "Are you serious?"

He scowled at her.

"God, Roarke, look at you. You're…" she borrowed his gesture and waved her hand in his direction.

"I'm…?" he prompted.

Muscled. Tatted. And sexy as hell. Just looking at him did things to her she didn't think possible.

"Hot. Trust me, no one is going to fuck you because they feel sorry for you." She sighed. "Do you know how long it's been since I had sex?"

"Marina—"

"Do you know the only man I've ever been with is my ex-husband? We met in high school. I never did the whole dating thing. He was my first boyfriend. My *only* boyfriend. I've never so much as kissed another man. Except for you."

And how pathetic did that sound?

He swallowed. "Not my problem."

She pulled at her bottom lip with her teeth, watched his dark gaze flare at the movement. "I ache, Roarke. I ache for someone to touch me, really touch me."

A pulse ticked at his temple, his jaw flexed. "I'm not that guy."

"So I should find someone else?"

CHAPTER FIVE

The shaft of whatever the fuck it was that scorched through him almost brought him to his knees. Marina. With some other guy doing what *he* wanted to do to her, what he'd imagined, over and over. He'd felt violent rage inside himself before, but it was nothing compared to this.

He clenched his jaw, tried to count off the reasons why it shouldn't have mattered to him.

He should make her walk away, turn her against him for good. If it were anyone else, it would be so fucking easy. He knew exactly what to do, what to say, but for some reason he couldn't do it. Not to Marina.

There was some protective instinct that kicked in for her, deep inside, a part of him he didn't think he had anymore for anyone other than family. He'd thought it long buried, but it was so strong it guaranteed her protection, even from himself.

"I can give myself an orgasm," she murmured. "But it's not enough. Not anymore. And I think there's only so many mediocre orgasms I can give myself."

Roarke closed his eyes, tried to get the images that punched into his head to go away.

"Fuck," he groaned. "I don't need that visual, okay?"

God, he was trying to do the right thing here. The right thing for her.

When he opened his eyes, she was looking at him, her gaze steady. Christ, her inexperience was obvious, so where the hell did that boldness come from?

Her bottom lip looked red where she'd bitten it. He wanted to lick at it, have her bite his lip like that. And only his.

"You won't go to anyone else to satisfy something—*anything*—that came from me. Got it?"

His voice came out rougher than he intended.

She stepped forward until she stood directly in front of him, so close he could feel the warmth from her body. He could smell her perfume. It was light and sexy at the same time and made him almost lightheaded.

"I haven't been with a woman in a hell of a long time."

Where had that come from? And what was it? A fucking disclaimer?

"How long exactly?"

He frowned. Who asked someone that? Apparently Marina did. He'd somehow given her the impression she could ask him whatever the fuck she wanted. Most people took the hint. No talking more than necessary and no personal questions. Ever. Not her.

"I don't know," he ground out. "I'm not keeping

track."

And why he always felt the need to answer her, he had no clue about that either.

She smiled. Soft and hot and condescending all at once. "Sure you are."

Yeah. Right. Of course. He had a pretty accurate idea of exactly how long it'd been and it was pathetic by anyone's standard.

"Enough. If we do this, we do it without all the getting-to-know-you bullshit."

God, was he really going to do this?

"Wow." Her eyebrows went sky high. "It must really be a long time."

"Marina—"

She laughed, the sound soft and warm. And foreign. "I'm teasing."

Teasing? Is that what she called it? She was driving him out of his Goddamn mind, whatever it was.

"It's going to be difficult with the crutches," he warned.

"I might know a thing or two about crutches. I think we can figure something out."

"I don't have any rubbers."

Christ, he couldn't remember the last time he'd bought any.

"I assumed BYO."

He groaned. "Do you have an answer for everything?"

"Nursing is kind of like being a Scout. You have to be prepared for anything."

What the fuck was he waiting for? Roarke tried to list off all the reasons why he had no business touching her, why he shouldn't take what she offered. Nothing made sense, nothing stuck. Nothing he came up with was enough to cancel out the hot, filthy images he had of her. Naked. Under him. Wet. Moaning. He screwed his eyes shut for an endless second. Tight. And coming.

"Just fucking," he ground out. "Nothing more. One time."

She wet her lips and nodded and he swore he almost felt that swipe of her tongue against his own lips, and lower, around the head of his cock.

"Know what I want?" he forced out, the blood a roar in his ears. "Right this minute?"

"What?"

"You. On your back. Coming because my mouth is between your legs."

Her eyes went wide and she trembled. Her saw her swallow.

Most people would have taken the hint and fucked off away from him by now. Not her. She seemed nervous, maybe even scared. Good. He was glad she was scared because the way she made him feel terrified the fuck out of him.

She was about to have sex with the hottest guy she'd ever seen.

She was about to have sex with the…

Oh God.

She was about to have sex.

Marina tried to take a big gulp of air, but it somehow got caught as a lump in her throat. And it did nothing to calm the rapid thudding of her heart. The beating was so fast, so loud, she might be in danger of passing out.

She snorted to herself. How would that look? At

the prospect of her first sex in six years and she fainted?

His room was clean and stark compared to the rest of the house, but God, it was still a mattress on the floor. It should have felt seedy and cheap, but it didn't. Anything but.

Roarke had locked up the house and maneuvered himself onto the bed. His hot gaze swept her from head to foot and she trembled from the intensity of it.

"You've already seen me naked," he drawled. "It hardly seems fair."

"That—that was in a professional capacity."

His mouth lifted at one corner. "Trust me, my dick didn't know the difference."

She shrugged off the nerves—or tried to— and kneeled on the mattress next to him. Before she could second-guess herself, she eased the shirt up over her head and off.

The fancy, lacy bra got a cursory glance.

"Considering how uncomfortable it is, you should probably lose the bra too," he murmured.

Her hands shook, but she unhooked the clasp and let the bra slide off her arms. God, she took off a bra every day. The move should have been smooth, easy. Instead it ended up being clumsy and awkward.

The cool air washed against the heated skin of her breasts and she felt her nipples harden. She was naked from the waist up, exposed, vulnerable, yet his eyes never left hers.

"You're nervous."

She swallowed again against the dryness of her throat. "Duh."

"Don't overthink it, Marina. It's just fucking."

She almost snorted at that. Right. She'd never

done the "just fucking" thing before.

Only then did his gaze drop. Heat exploded inside her when he pulled at his bottom lip with his teeth while he took his time looking at her. The move was sexy and hot and told her he liked what he saw. More than liked.

He sat up in a surge of movement and tugged off his t-shirt with a rough hand at the back of his neck. The move was fluid and coordinated and screamed male confidence. No awkwardness there.

The muscles, the tattoos, the scars. The sharp punch to her gut told her she was finally going to be able to get her hands on all of it. Maybe her mouth. Large expanses of smooth skin, covered with dark, stark tattoos. All hers to explore. To kiss. To lick.

He tipped her chin up so that her eyes were on his. "Marina, are you sure you—"

"God. *Yes*. I'm just…a little overwhelmed." She swallowed. "Continue."

His mouth lifted at one corner. "You're bossy. Anyone ever tell you that?"

"All the time. It comes in handy when dealing with rude, difficult patients."

His gaze drifted down again and he licked his lips. "I'm going to tell you everything I'm going to do, okay?"

She nodded and then realized he couldn't see it.

"Okay," she whispered.

"I want to kiss you. And not on the lips."

Oh. God.

Because he was looking at her chest. He eased her onto her back, somehow ended up on top of her, between her legs. He propped himself above her with a forearm next to her head and eased her legs wide with his thick thighs.

She could feel him through her skirt and his jeans, solid and unyielding.

She gasped when he lowered his head to her and licked her nipple with a bold, sure swipe. He pulled it into his mouth, sucking and tugging until she felt the suckling sensation between her legs, right where she ached, throbbed.

"Too much?" he murmured. His warm breath fanned her wet nipple and she shivered at the sensation.

"I… What—what was that? That thing you did, with your— What—"

"You mean this?"

He bent to her other nipple, his hot mouth closing over it completely, while he licked and flicked and rolled her nipple with his tongue. Maybe his teeth. It could have been both.

She bit her lip against the pleasure that seared a path straight down, exploding low in her abdomen and lower.

When he eased back, his gaze dropped right down where she ached, where she was hot and wet, as if he knew exactly where she'd felt the suction of his mouth.

"And when I get my mouth between your legs?"

His voice was low and rough and rumbled across nerve endings already heightened. "That's exactly the move I'm going to use against your clit."

Dear. God. In. Heaven.

He trailed his hot, open mouth down between her breasts and lower, the sensation of the rasp of his beard against her already sensitized skin making her gasp and tremble under him. Of course, the trembling might be because of what he was about to do, what she was about to experience.

Stuart had gone down on her, of course he had. Honestly, it'd been...okay—she guessed—except she didn't think it was supposed to only feel "okay". Somehow she knew when Roarke went down on her, it wasn't going to be the same, not even in the same ballpark.

He eased his big body down over hers, lifting his mouth when he got to the skirt. A rough hand slid up her thigh and under the fabric until he'd bunched it at her waist. Cool air washed against heated skin. The muscles in her stomach jerked in anticipation when he inched the top of her panties down. And stopped.

He leaned in close, so close she could feel his hot breath against the skin of her stomach. "What's this?"

She sighed. It'd been bound to come up, but God, did it have to be when he'd been about to rock her world? "C-section scar."

His gaze lifted to hers, his brows low over his eyes. "You didn't tell me you had a kid."

"Does it matter?"

"No," he bit out.

"Then what's the problem?"

He hesitated for an endless second. "I don't do the whole kid thing."

Yeah, it wouldn't be the first time she'd heard that. "I don't do the whole prospective dad thing either, so..."

She'd never wanted to expose Sam to another man. Ever.

"I'm not looking for a potential father for Samantha. I'm not even looking for a relationship. At all. Probably ever."

"Then what?"

She swallowed. "You know what. Touch. Pleasure. I…"

"That I can guarantee."

God. Confident much? She jumped when he bent and closed his mouth over her through her panties, arching against the heat of his mouth, the pressure of his tongue, shivering when he scored her with his teeth.

"You smell fucking incredible."

He yanked her panties down her thighs, as far as they could go with her legs wedged open and put his mouth to her again, this time without any barrier. Only hot, wet heat.

He licked her with bold, thick strokes, sucking gently against her until she couldn't hold in the moan that tore from her. It was low and loud and she was pretty sure she'd never made a sound like that before. The scrape of his soft beard against her thighs, the sensitive flesh between her legs, heightened everything his tongue and teeth and lips were doing.

Marina sucked in a breath, another, but nothing helped, she couldn't get enough air, couldn't catch her breath, couldn't control the flood of sensation that threatened to engulf her, drown her.

She rocked her hips into his mouth, the movements frenzied and uncoordinated, but she didn't care. She threaded fingers into his hair to hold him to her. His tongue flicked against her clit, over and over until she couldn't do anything but put her head back, close her eyes and give herself over to him.

She whimpered, tried to move back from the intensity, the pressure, the pain of pleasure. He spread his fingers wide over her abdomen, holding her back down against the mattress, holding her still for his mouth so that she couldn't escape his relentless tongue. Not that she wanted to. Not really.

The orgasm when it came was hard and intense. And over way too fast. The sharp slam of pleasure burned through her like wildfire, but her legs kept shaking and she couldn't make them stop. Because it hadn't been enough. Not even close.

She opened her eyes as Roarke yanked at the opening of his jeans, shoved them and his underwear down his legs and kicked them off.

His eyes were dark, his cheeks flushed, his features drawn in hard lines of stark need. And his lips. They were wet. With her.

And then the shaking had no chance of stopping. Because he was naked. All the way naked with that hard, honed body and flexing muscles.

Oh. God.

If a guy's penis could be perfectly formed, his was. It was long and thick, smooth and—she swallowed—hard.

His mouth kicked up at the corner. "I thought you said you'd seen plenty before? In fact, you've probably seen a bunch today already. Am I right?"

"Yes, but..." She licked her dry lips. "Not, you know, like that. Of course, some patients get erect. I told you that, right? But it's... Well, they're not usually..."

"What?"

"So... big."

Roarke choked out a sound.

"Or, you know...thick." Her eyes dropped to his dick again. "Or smooth looking and—"

"Okay, I got it."

"Or about to be deep inside me."

"Marina," he groaned.

He tugged her panties the rest of the way off and grabbed the rubber she'd given him. He rolled it on with an economy of movement that told her all she needed to know about his level of experience. As if she'd needed any further proof after the tongue action. Even with the rubber on he looked—

"It'll fit."

Her gaze shot up to meet his and heat rushed into her cheeks. The lopsided smile was sexy and sinister all at once and made him look younger.

"You can read minds too?"

"Only yours."

Marina gulped when he moved up and over her again. She loved his thighs. They were thick and heavily muscled. Sprinkled with dark hair. Like tree trunks only hella sexy. And when he pushed her legs wide with them… Oh yeah.

She clutched at him, at his massive biceps as he braced himself over her. His muscles were so solid, her nails barely made any dent.

This was happening. To her. Right now.

"Marina."

She opened eyes she hadn't been aware she'd screwed shut. He was close, so close she could see each of his eyelashes, the different-colored blues in his eyes, the tiny scar above his eyebrow she'd never noticed before.

"Breathe."

She let out a long breath and then sucked in another when he eased into her an inch.

"Okay?"

She nodded.

He stretched her—slow, careful—until he was deep. She sighed at the sliding pressure, the pleasure that followed, so intense she wanted to close her eyes and revel in it. But she wanted to watch him more. The way his eyelids flickered with his own pleasure. The way his jaw clenched each time he'd pushed forward. The way his gaze hadn't left hers.

He moved his hips a fraction. She whimpered at the shaft of pleasure that radiated deep inside and he stilled.

"It's…"

There was no way she could get any words out, no way she could even put into words the sensations that coursed through her.

"Yeah," he bit out. "I know."

She shifted her hips, a test, but it caused him to move against her, deep inside. "You—you're bigger than my husband."

His eyes narrowed. "A suggestion? You don't mention him, you don't even think about him, when I'm inside you. Deal?"

She nodded, couldn't do anything else at the deep, dark look in his eyes.

"And he's your fucking *ex*."

"Roarke—"

"No more talking."

It was impossible anyway, because he started to move, deep, even strokes that stretched her wide with each inward thrust and had her own hips rising to meet his.

Marina gripped his massive biceps. "Slow—slow down," she gasped.

He stilled above her. "Why?"

"I—I want to savor the sensations, I want to be

able to remember what everything feels like, I—"

"Marina," he groaned. "It's getting to the point where I won't be able to slow down so tell me right now if you're with me or not."

She licked her dry lips. "I am. I so am. But—but I'm close." She closed her eyes, tried to take a breath, tried to stop her body from flexing around him. He sucked in a breath when she failed. "I just… I just want it to last."

There was no telling when she'd ever get another chance like this. With a guy who was built like he was. She still felt stretched to the max, impaled on his thick length. Who wouldn't want that to last? And who could blame a girl for wanting to imprint it on her memory so she could play it over and over in her mind later?

She gasped when he ground his hips against her, pressing against some place inside her nothing and no one had ever found before.

She trembled when he lowered his lips to her ear and his hot breath fanned against her cheek, down her neck.

"No one said you only get to come once."

Oh God.

"But we'll take it slow."

"Okay," she managed. She sighed, her breath fluttering out on a shaky exhale.

"Next time."

Her stomach clenched. "But you said—"

He pulled out and then slid back in, all the way, the thrust causing her to tense and whimper.

"Neither of us believed me when I said we'd only do this once. Not really. And now? I haven't come yet, but I know when I do, it's going to blow the top of my fucking head off."

Marina didn't know what to do, she couldn't think, only feel. So she did what she could, which was gripping him hard, panting so that she could get enough air, and moaning "Oh God" over and over in time to his heavy thrusts into her.

Roarke screwed his eyes shut tight, tried to think about something mundane, boring, anything to cancel out the sensation of the tight, hot clasp of her body around his cock.

He felt the tingle at the base of his spine, the tightening in his balls and knew he was close. So fucking close. But there was no way he was going to let go, not until she came screaming his name. Actually, he'd settle for just the coming part. And hoped it was soon.

He looked down at her. Big mistake. Her eyes were almost all the way closed as if she could barely keep them open and God, those whimpers.

She was so fucking gorgeous, nothing held back in her expression. He couldn't wait to watch her when she came because it was going to be fucking epic. Almost from the first moment he'd seen her, he'd imagined this, fantasized about it. Marina. Under him. Taking him deep.

She was looking at him through her lashes. He didn't usually like being watched, but from her it was a turn on, ramping up his hunger, his need to pleasure her.

He fought the urge to thrust harder, to use his thighs to nudge her legs farther apart, to pound into her faster.

Shit just got real because he really wasn't sure how much longer he could last. He eased himself up, draped her legs over his thighs, hoping like hell the visual stimulation alone wasn't enough to send him over because in this position he could see both the soft jiggle of her tits and his cock sliding in and out of her.

He used his thumb to rub over her clit, spreading her moisture over the tight nub, bit back a groan when she tightened around him.

"*Roarke.*"

"I'm here," he managed. Barely. He was holding on by a fucking thread. Maybe a miracle.

"I'm…"

She bit her lip, threw her head back, arched up against him.

Fuck. Yeah.

She was going to come and he had a first-row seat. He clenched his jaw, locked his back teeth together and kept his thrusts steady, picking up the pace a fraction when she moaned.

Her body fisted around him. Hard. He gasped at the sensation, his thrusts faltering for a split second until her hips began pistoning against him, jerky and uncoordinated, until her legs began to tremble.

How he held it, he'll never know. It helped that she'd dug her fingers into his side. The pain was sharp. And welcome. He gritted his teeth and thrust through her orgasm, watched her face as pleasure burst through her, on and on, as her body convulsed under and around him.

It was the most beautiful thing he'd ever seen.

His hands were shaking. Fuck, his whole body was shaking, balanced on the knife-edge of something he knew he'd never experienced before. He waited until her breathing slowed, until her eyes started to open before he grasped her hips hard and rolled with her until she was on top of him.

The move sent him deep. She put her hands on his chest for balance, dug her nails into the muscles there as she sat up.

"God, Roarke, that was…"

Yeah. Fucking incredible was what it was.

He smoothed unsteady hands down each of her firm thighs, bit back a savage smile when she sucked in a breath. Her hair was tangled, her cheeks flushed, her eyes dark and dazed with pleasure, the hard points of her nipples a deep red.

She looked as if she'd been well-fucked. And beautiful. So beautiful.

Every muscle in his body was held tight, as if something was going to break at any minute. And maybe it was. The level of control he needed not to give in and drive into her uncontrollably—taking his own release—might just kill him. But he'd damn well wait until she caught up again.

All at once she frowned. "You didn't—"

"No," he ground out. "You don't get to come just once, remember?"

"Oh, Roarke," she sighed.

"I need…"

God, what did he need? He needed to come. He needed to explode with her heat around him. And yeah, if it made him an arrogant ass that he wanted to make her come again for him, so be it.

She bit her lip, used her leverage on his chest to move against him. It was tentative, exploratory, but he was way past the point of being teased.

"Move." A low groan he had no hope of holding back was torn from him. "God, *move.*"

That was as much as he could manage. He crushed his fingers into the soft flesh of her hips and guided her movements until she was sliding along his length, hot and tight.

She sucked in a harsh breath when he found her clit with his thumb again. He rubbed, flicking back and forth, controlling the pressure until she started to pant. Her lids drifted closed and God, she started to make those whimpering sounds that meant she was close.

And then her features tightened, her body freezing for an endless second before she moaned, convulsing hard around him. Again.

Only when he knew for absolute sure she was coming, did he let go. He clasped her hips in rough hands, screwed his eyes shut and slammed up into her, once, twice, a third time before he exploded, long and deep, throbs of pleasure so intense it felt like pain sizzled through every nerve ending in his body.

He groaned, flipped her over until she was sprawled under him, driving into her hard, over and over, until the pulses finally stopped, until the roaring in his ears quietened, until he could finally string a coherent thought together.

Roarke blinked, tried to control his breathing, the thundering of his heart that threatened to burst from his chest. He hated not being one hundred percent aware of his surroundings at all times and in those few seconds of mindless, powerful pleasure he hadn't been. He hadn't taken so much as a fucking aspirin in years, not willingly, yet Marina just might be the most potent drug he'd ever experienced.

She'd stripped him down until he was raw and open and he didn't like it. Not one bit.

He'd wanted hard and fast and impersonal. Instead, it'd been anything but. And fuck…missionary? He'd never thought he'd get so worked up over straight-up, vanilla sex. But it'd felt right. With her.

Her legs were still wrapped around him, still trembling, tiny movements he could feel against his thighs. The scene of their sex hung heavy in the air and he fought the urge to inhale, to inhale her. Instead, he forced himself to pull out, gritting his teeth as her body clenched around him when he withdrew.

"You okay?"

She was still fighting for breath, hadn't opened her eyes yet.

"Marina?"

"It…didn't suck." Her voice was hoarse, low, the words sounding as if they were forced out.

He frowned. That was it? Was he that far out of the loop that he wasn't good at this anymore? She'd come that time, he was sure of it. Right?

"What—"

"I—I just need a minute."

She opened her eyes, but turned her head to the side rather than look at him.

A minute?

"For what?"

He grasped her chin, turned her back to him. Had he been too rough, too fast, too…something?

"Marina…"

Everything in him stilled when her eyes lifted to meet his.

"I didn't know sex could be like that, okay?" she whispered.

"Like what?"

But he knew. Mixed in with the satisfaction, she looked as shell-shocked as he felt. And it shouldn't have been like that. He shouldn't have felt anything beyond a physical release. So, okay, he'd known that release was going to be fucking epic, but dammit he shouldn't be…*feeling*.

"Like—like… Oh God." She sighed—slow and soft—and the sensation went straight to his dick. Which should have been impossible.

"You never said if we screw and it blows *my* mind, that I couldn't call *you*. Right?"

He felt some of the tension ease from his muscles. How did she do that? Tie him up in knots and then unravel him just as fast?

It'd been the best sex he'd ever had—hands down. And not because it'd been so long since he'd been with a woman. Not because he'd been primed to go off like a fucking rocket. Not because he barely remembered what it felt like to come anywhere else except in his Goddamn hand. No. It was because of *her*. She'd crawled in under his leave-me-the-fuck-alone armor when he wasn't looking. This thing they had? Yeah, he'd be an idiot to think it was merely physical. The problem was how the hell did he get her back out while he still had the chance?

BREAK DOWN

CHAPTER SIX

Marina's eyes snapped open. Her heart was pounding, her breathing fast, erratic. It was dark, quiet in her room, so why the hell was she wide awake at—she glanced over at the clock—two-eighteen?

Thunk.

She frowned. Was that what had woken her?

Thunk. Thunk.

There it was again. She sat up, tried to place the sound. It almost sounded as if... God, why would someone be chopping wood? In her back yard?

She grabbed a robe, slipping her phone into the pocket. After making sure Sam was still sleeping, she moved through the dark house to the back door. She looked out the kitchen window, but didn't have a clear view of her backyard, not where the wood pile was anyway.

Thunk.

Marina kept her steps quiet, tried not to think about every horror movie she'd ever seen, tried to convince herself that she wasn't the dumb chick who should have stayed inside and called the police.

She froze in place when she rounded the corner of the house. Even in the shadows she could see it was Roarke, naked to the waist, making each swing of the axe look effortless. An axe that wasn't hers.

She'd only seen him once all week and that'd been from a distance. He'd arrived when the roof repairs were finished, inspecting as much of the work as he could without getting up on the ladder. Even on crutches he'd made a commanding figure and it'd been clear the roofing guys respected the hell out of him. His dark gaze had met hers once—sizzling and bold—before he'd left without a word.

She'd thought sex with Roarke would have been wild and rough, untamed. He'd been confident, dominating and forceful, but every touch had been gentle. He'd been so focused on her, so careful of her pleasure, so determined. Who would have guessed a man that hard, that strong, that…savage to everyone around him, was capable of that level of tenderness?

Of course, she'd never had sex like that, figured great sex was either a lie or just something she wasn't likely to experience for herself. One of those one-in-a-million things. Things that happened to other people.

"Thanks," he muttered, without looking at her, bending to put another log up on the stump.

She'd never seen anyone chop wood using a single crutch for balance before. She guessed Roarke had probably figured out how to do a lot of things with crutches no else would attempt. She'd tried several times to make some of the logs into useable firewood. Each time she'd given up.

"For?"

She wrapped the robe more securely around her and crossed her arms. It wasn't really cold, but there was a gentle breeze and she hadn't put any shoes on. Her toes were starting to go numb.

"For not asking me what I'm doing," he rasped. "It's pretty fucking obvious."

He swung the axe in a smooth arc, splitting the wood in to two even pieces. The muscles under the smooth skin of his back and arms slid and flexed with the effort.

"So why are you out here in the middle of the night doing that which is pretty fucking obvious?"

He picked up the halves, tossed them onto the pile that was almost as high as her waist.

"These logs are too big to use in the fireplace."

Right. Of course. She knew that, had tried the whole chopping thing a few times herself. It was way harder than it looked, which is why she'd resorted to buying wood at the store when she wanted to light the fire. Which wasn't very often. Because she had to buy logs from the store.

His movements were almost mesmerizing to watch, controlled and powerful. He made it look so easy.

"Don't you dare," she warned when one downward swing of the axe had him rebalancing the crutch.

"What?"

"Fall. There's no way I'd be able to lift you up."

He choked out a sound that could have been a laugh, his version of one anyway. He bent to set another large log on the block.

"Roarke."

He ignored her, swung the axe down. She stepped

in front of him after he'd tossed the pieces out of the way, so close he couldn't do anything else but look at her.

"You gonna swear at me?" he bit out.

"If I need to."

He glanced down, frowned when he noticed the bat she held in her hand.

"You came out here in the dark by yourself with a fucking baseball bat?"

"No. It's a softball bat."

His lips tightened and his dark brows shot low over eyes. "I could have been anyone."

She tilted her head to the side. "I don't think a peeping Tom would want to make sure I was prepared for winter."

"Marina—"

"Why are you here, Roarke?"

He huffed out a breath. "Couldn't sleep."

"So you decided to come chop my wood?"

His wiped his forehead with a rough sweep of his forearm. "I noticed the pile when I was here before. Seemed like a good idea at the time."

"In the middle of the night."

"Like I said, I couldn't sleep."

"Why not?"

He looked down then. Her eyes widened when he flipped the sharp axe end-over-end, the handle landing in his palm with deadly precision. "Yeah, that you don't want to know."

"Roarke—"

"Look, I usually run, okay? I trash the treadmill or hit the streets."

Okay. And neither were an option right now.

"Come inside, Roarke."

God, she hadn't meant it as a double entendre. She hadn't. But when his gaze locked to hers, heat speared out from *there*, right where her dirty mind was already imaging him—his mouth, his fingers, his impressive cock.

Heat flooded her face.

"I'm not here for sex," he ground out.

"Right. You came to…" she made finger quotes with her hands, "chop wood."

Even in the low light she could see his mouth lift at one corner. He glanced back toward the house.

"Where's your kid?"

"Asleep. She won't wake up. She sleeps like the dead."

He was silent for a heartbeat, two. "I'll leave right after."

She let out an unsteady breath, gave a rueful smile. She wouldn't have expected anything else.

* * * * *

Marina closed the door to her room, leaned back against it. Her heartbeat was racing so fast and so loud, he could probably hear it.

He hadn't bothered putting his shirt back on and he threw it onto the foot of her bed. Holy hell, but his back was a thing of beauty—smooth, muscled, powerful.

He stopped in front of the big chair by her bed and turned, flipping the crutches upside down and leaning them against the wall.

Marina took a deep, steadying breath. It didn't help much. Maybe not at all. Her gaze dropped. He was hard, straining the confines of the denim.

There was no hesitation, no modesty. He jerked at the opening of his jeans, yanking them down with his underwear. He sat on the chair and leaned back, muscled thighs spread wide, his cock thick and long against his stomach.

Oh God.

"Take off the robe."

Cursing the tremors in her hands, Marina shrugged off the robe and let it drop to the floor. She was wearing men's pajama bottoms and a tank top, yet from the hot, explicit look in his eyes it could have been the sexiest lingerie.

"The pants too."

She swallowed against her dry throat and tugged off the pants, kicking them aside.

"Leave it," he rasped, as she grabbed the hem of her tank top. "I want to take it off."

He held out a hand and her heart thundered so hard it was almost deafening. She stepped forward and his hard hands bracketed her hips, eased her down and over him until she sat, straddling his lap, the hair on his thighs rasping against the sensitive flesh of her inner legs. She shivered at the sensation.

"Christ, look at you."

Rough fingers grasped the bottom of her tank top, dragging it up, slow, agonizingly slow, until she felt the cool air against her nipples.

"I need to taste."

Oh God.

He bent, licked first one nipple, teasing, taunting licks, then the other, alternating between them until she couldn't help the involuntary movements of her lower body against his thighs. He wasn't sucking hard, pulling or biting at them. He didn't use his hands, only his mouth, and he was lapping at her, mindless flicks and licks and it sent a shaft of pure sensation straight to her clit. It felt as if the smallest touch from him there and it'd be game over.

"I can feel how hot and wet you are against me," he rasped.

So could she.

"Put your knees up on the arms of the chair."

"I—what?"

He urged her up until she knelt on each of the thick, sturdy arms. She gasped when his hands cupped the curves of her ass, sliding down to the crease between.

Was he trembling? She thought she felt it in the hands holding her, but it could have come from her.

One hand trailed around her hip and she jumped when he rubbed a thumb back and forth across her soaked clit. She throbbed, ached, burned and then she couldn't think, could only feel, as he inserted a thick finger inside her.

"Roarke," she moaned and flexed involuntarily around him.

He groaned, his gaze fixed between her legs, watching her, watching his finger as he moved it slowly in and out of her, retreating all the way and then sinking back in.

His nostrils flared. "*Fuck*. You always smell incredible."

Before she could guess his intention he leaned forward and put his mouth against her.

Her whole body jerked at the contact. Fighting for breath, struggling for some semblance of sanity, Marina looked down. His eyes, dark and raw, were watching her, causing a heat she'd never experienced before to burn through her.

Marina ground herself against him, pushed herself hard against his mouth, his tongue, God, that finger.

All at once he grasped her hips and lifted her away from his mouth, down so that she straddled him again. Cool air washed against flesh that was hot, wet and aching. She'd been so close. She had to bite her lip to stop herself from begging him to continue, offering him anything if he'd just do it again, but he was already ripping open the condom packet.

"Hurry," she whispered, her voice ragged, as she eased back on his thighs to give him room.

He rolled the condom on with sharp, jerky moves. She'd never watched a guy put one on before Roarke. She liked it. A lot. Maybe it should have been a turn-off, but Roarke? Touching himself? Yeah, she might just go up in flames at how hot and dirty it made her feel.

"I want to watch it go in," he grated.

She positioned herself over him, her legs shaking with need. He grasped his cock and rubbed himself back and forth through her slick folds, applying just enough pressure to have her gasping and rocking against him. She gripped his thick shoulders for balance, wanting to slam herself down onto him, but he held her hips, controlled his entry.

"Easy," he rasped.

He thrust up against her, slow and shallow, patient. She whimpered at the sensation of stretching, her moisture slowly easing his path, his thickness a living brand inside her. All at once she wanted more, she wanted all of him, as much of him as she could take.

"Roarke please, *please*—"

He groaned and eased his hold on her hips. She

sank down onto him, bit by bit, filling herself with his broad length. She sucked in a breath, felt her wet heat flex and clench around him when he was deep.

"Move."

His voice was harsh, barely recognizable, his features drawn in hard lines. Marina used the leverage from his shoulders to lift her body, to rock herself on him. Sweet, searing sensation—so good it almost felt like pain—surged through her as she repeated the move, over and over, with frenzied jerks of her hips.

She whimpered as her body went taut, froze for an endless second as pleasure burst and full-body tremors raged through her.

Roarke groaned, low and deep, his hot breath fanning her breasts, pulling her body down onto him, hard, while he thrust under her with powerful movements of his hips, pistoning his body into hers through her orgasm.

"Holy shit," he managed after they were both still, the sound of their ragged breathing loud in the quiet room.

Yeah.

She opened eyes and saw the fingers of her hand clenched in the back of the arm chair, the one she'd inherited from her great-aunt. She blew back a strand of hair that had fallen across her eyes.

One thing was certain. She was never going to be able to sit in this chair again and not remember what she'd done in it.

* * * * *

Roarke opened his eyes, keeping the rest of his body still. It was a habit ingrained in him that he'd never been able to break, not even after all this time—to wake and assess the surroundings for risk before making his consciousness known.

He knew in an instant it was late. And that he wasn't in his own bed, but in a chair.

He'd dressed—after—ready to leave, except he hadn't. He'd stayed to watch Marina sleep for a few minutes and...

Fuck.

He'd never done that before, fallen so deeply asleep in a strange place. Spent the night with a woman. Slept—he glanced at his watch—shit, for a straight four hours.

Marina was still sleeping, her breathing soft and even. She lay on her stomach, only partly covered. The sheet had slipped down or she'd kicked it off and he had a full view of her naked back and curvy ass. And the dark, shadowed cleft between.

He wanted to crawl into bed with her, over her. Hell, he wanted to yank the sheet down all the way, spread her ass cheeks wide and plow into her from behind until the mindless pleasure she could create in him rolled over him. He wanted to see her body stretch to accommodate him, watch her ass wiggle, her legs tremble as she came. He wanted to hear those soft sounds she made when he entered her.

He hadn't come here last night for sex. He hadn't. Although what she could do to him beat out any amount of thrashing he could give his treadmill.

He rubbed his hand down over his face. He needed a shower and coffee—bad—and not necessarily in that order. And he needed to get his ass back to work. He also had a doctor's appointment, which meant he might be able to finally ditch the crutches.

He kept his movements light, shut the bedroom door carefully behind him and turned to go.

Aw, crap.

She had Marina's eyes. The same color, the same shape and that same calm way of looking at him.

"Hey," he offered in greeting.

Christ, what did you say to a kid anyway? What did *he*? Especially one who'd caught him sneaking out of her Mom's bedroom.

"Hey."

She nodded, waited. For what?

"Um..."

God, she was just a kid. Why was his stomach tied in knots all of a sudden?

She tilted her head to the side. "My name's Samantha, but I like Sam better. Yeah, I'm cute." She rolled her eyes. "I'm nine. My Dad's not here."

When Roarke frowned, she shrugged.

"People always ask me where my Dad is when I'm not with my Mom."

Oh, did they? Yeah, he guessed they figured they could pump a kid for information to satisfy their curiosity. Fuckers.

"Why don't you tell them to mind their own business?" he drawled.

When her eyebrows went high, he cleared his throat. "Just...you know, maybe in a nicer way than that."

Christ, he of all people should *not* be giving a kid advice.

"Do you want to know where he is?"

"No."

"Why not?"

"If I did, I'd ask your Mom. Just like everyone else should."

He had no right to be around kids for God's sake. She stood looking at him, calm, waiting. Again. For what?

"Okay." She sighed and started counting off on her fingers. "I'm nine. And a half. Yes, I know I look like my Mom. I like to read and play softball. No, I don't like school. Mainly because it's boring."

Gutsy and matter-of-fact. Just like Marina.

"Get tired of being asked the same questions all the time, huh?"

She rolled her eyes again. "You have no idea."

He fought a smile and lost.

"Well, I'm Roarke. I'm...a friend of your Mom's. I'm way older than nine and I like to work with my hands, to make things. I never liked school either, mainly because I was never any good at it."

"Can you do hair?"

"Do...hair?"

What did that even mean?

"You said you were good with your hands. Mommy can't hardly even do a ponytail."

"Ah..."

"I'm hungry. I can show you where everything is in the kitchen."

There was a clear expectation there. The kid was fully dressed, shoes and all. He looked back toward the bedroom door. Did he really want the kid to go in there and find Marina naked? Probably not.

"Ah...okay, but my ability to make food is limited to what I eat," he warned.

She nodded and Roarke followed her down the hall and into the kitchen at the back of the house. It was clean and light. Everything was original to the house and the appliances had seen better days. Probably about ten years ago.

He opened the fridge, wondering how the hell he'd agreed to get a kid breakfast. Eggs. Juice. Easy. Seemed like a good start. He was hungry himself.

"What happened to your leg?"

He leaned one of the crutches against the cabinet so he could maneuver better in the same space.

"Long story."

He glanced at her when she didn't say anything else. She looked at him for so long, Roarke was back to wondering what the fuck to say, to do.

"You have scared eyes," she whispered.

Scared? Not scary? That one he'd heard before.

"Yeah? There's a lot of scary stuff in the world, kid."

He had no clue what she meant, except that this tiny person, who looked and sounded so much like Marina, pretty much terrified the crap out of him.

* * * * *

Shit.

Marina skidded to a stop when she got to the kitchen, her heart still beating so fast she was breathless from it after she'd found Sam's bed empty.

Sam was sitting at the breakfast bar next to Roarke, her pose an exact replica of his—legs spread wide on the stool, one ankle resting on a knee. Eating scrambled eggs. Her daughter had never eaten scrambled eggs before in her life, had refused to even try them.

Oh boy.

She'd never dated, had never introduced any man to her daughter before and had certainly never had one stay the night. And God, she'd assumed—expected—Roarke would have been long gone.

"Wow, that is so cool."

Marina couldn't see what her daughter was looking at, but her heart skipped a beat at the smile in her voice.

"Can you show *me* how to do it?"

"Ah…"

She never got to hear what Roarke's response would have been. Sam's arm swung wide, reaching across to Roarke for something and hit a glass, knocking it over and spilling juice all over the breakfast bar.

Marina stood frozen, watching the sticky liquid drip down onto the floor and onto Roarke's thigh.

Sam jumped down off the stool, eyes wide, horrified, as Roarke righted the glass.

"I'm sorry." Her voice was high, panicked almost. "I didn't mean it."

"It's just an accident, kid. You okay?"

Roarke's works were calm, even, yet still Sam waited and Marina's heart clenched. Stuart was always impatient with her if she spilled or broke something and she'd come to expect his annoyance, even his anger.

Marina was just about to step forward and intervene when Roarke turned on the stool to face Sam.

"What do you normally do if you make a mess?"

Her still wide eyes dropped to the dark patch on his jeans. "But—"

"I can't tell you it doesn't matter if you screw up,

but what matters more is how you fix it."

Sam gave a serious nod and went to the roll of paper towels Marina kept on the countertop near the sink. Marina stood—mesmerized—while Sam wiped up the juice, frowning in concentration as she made sure she got every last drop.

The surface would have to be wiped down again to get rid of the stickiness, but Jeez, did she just get a parenting lesson from Roarke?

He glanced up then, his searing gaze sweeping her from head to foot in a look she knew missed nothing. God, she was a mess. She'd stopped just long enough to yank on her robe and that was it.

He got up from the stool and grabbed the crutch he'd propped next to him.

His powerful body—honed and rugged in the faded jeans and close-fitting black t-shirt—dominated the space in her small kitchen. And one simple look from him and she was right back there again, against him, over him. She bit her lip at the heat that surged through her, at the images that threatened to burn her alive.

"I saved it!" Sam exclaimed, holding up a figure. "Mommy, look what Roarke made."

Marina stepped forward and frowned. It looked like a dragon made out of the notepaper she used for her grocery lists.

"That's incredible," she breathed. The detail was amazing, intricate folds and layers creating a 3-D form that looked exactly like a miniature dragon, wings and all.

She caught his gaze. "How did you do that?"

He shrugged as if it were nothing.

"I—"

She broke off when the doorbell rang and almost groaned out loud. Stuart might miss the mark on a lot of things, but he was always on time.

"Sam—"

"I know. I know. I'll go get my bag." She waved the dragon up above her head as she skipped off. "Thank you, Roarke."

"Roarke, I—"

The doorbell rang again and she sighed.

"Um...excuse me," she muttered.

God, awkward much? Marina tied the robe more tightly around her waist before she opened the door.

Stuart had his hands thrust into the pockets of his perfectly pressed khakis, impatience stamped on his features. She'd once thought him so handsome. Now he just seemed too polished, too smooth, too...uptight.

"Stuart. Sam's just getting her things."

"Marina." His expression said she'd looked better. Way better. Lucky for her she didn't care what he thought anymore.

He cleared his throat. "I wanted to let you know that after this weekend, I might not be able to take Sam for a while."

"What?" Was he kidding? "How long is 'awhile'?"

"I'm not sure. A few months perhaps, just until—"

"A few months? It's her birthday in three weeks. Did you even remember? What am I supposed to tell her? That you're too busy?"

He sighed, shook his head. "I knew you'd be difficult."

"Difficult?" she almost choked out.

He glanced back toward his car parked out front.

"Caroline wants me to spend more time with her and the baby."

"So? You have two children, Stuart. You barely see Sam now."

God, it was called fucking responsibility. She wanted to yell it at him, but then he'd complain about her language and lack of "class".

"Jim stepped out of the practice. I'm working a lot of extra hours right now to pick up the slack until we bring someone else on. Caroline wants a vacation place, another baby and…"

"So?"

She didn't know who the fuck Jim was and didn't care. And that was her problem…how?

"So cut me some slack here. I've got a lot of balls in the air right now."

Yeah, one of them was a membership to an exclusive country club. And let's not forget the brand new Mercedes.

She'd chosen wrong, so wrong. For her. And God…for Sam. She'd been seduced by his charm and his pretty words and his confidence in knowing who he was and what he wanted to do with his life. Unfortunately, it looked as if that hadn't involved either of them long-term.

She pitched her voice low. "This is probably the shittiest thing you've ever done, Stuart. And you've done a lot of shitty things."

His mouth curled in distaste. "I see your language hasn't improved."

"Everything okay?"

Marina sucked in a quick breath at the deep voice at her back. Roarke stood directly behind her, his dark eyes steady on Stuart. He held himself still, a leashed predatory power in every line of his body. His presence and two words, just two words from him, and some of the tension eased out of her shoulders.

She nodded.

"I need to get going," he added. "You sure?"

God, how did he do that? Make her feel safe and protected and hot and bothered all at once? Next to him Stuart seemed weak and whiny and... Well, just weak.

"Yeah. Thanks."

He inclined his head and eased past her, his big body brushing against hers. She had an instant of hard heat before it was gone.

Marina hid a smile at the look on Stuart's face, especially when Roarke pushed past him—forcing him to take his hands out of his pockets and step back.

The crutches should have made him seem awkward, but even they couldn't detract from the lean power of his body, the easy, fluid way he moved.

Stuart watched him until he got to the sidewalk. "Who's that?"

She ignored the question. "You know, Stuart, I've been meaning to apologize to you about something."

His gaze snapped to hers. He frowned. "For what exactly?"

Yeah, he'd know she really didn't have anything to be sorry for.

"For not being more understanding when you tried to explain to me what you saw in Caroline, what you'd found with her, how it was between the two of you."

"Ah..."

"How what we had had been so...routine, vanilla.

Boring."

He shifted from one foot to the other. "I... I never actually said that."

It was close enough. And it'd hurt, more than she'd ever admit. Stuart might have been a self-absorbed sexist asshole, but he'd been right all along about something. He'd even used it as justification for his fucking around. Their sex really had been unexciting, uninteresting and downright boring.

"Anyway, you were right. I didn't have any context back then. I had absolutely no idea sex could be so...*good*."

Amazing. Intense. Earth-shattering.

"Wait a minute. You—you're sleeping with someone?" He turned, motioned toward Roarke getting into a beaten-up pickup. "With *him*?"

For a doctor he could be really slow.

"You have responsibilities," he sputtered. "A child to raise."

Right. She decided not to point out that that child wasn't just hers.

"So?" she said yet again.

"So what kind of example are you setting for her by having a guy like that around?"

A guy like that? Hot? Ripped? Hung? Good with kids even if he didn't know it? Marina leaned forward so there was no way Sam could hear her.

"And what kind of example did you set by fucking everything with a vagina at the hospital while we were still married?"

CHAPTER SEVEN

Roarke put down the drywall sander and wiped his forearm across his forehead. The crew had already left for the day and he was beat. He stretched, wincing at the twinge in his side. He'd been sanding like a maniac for what seemed like hours to have the walls ready for paint and they were all done. Finally. Thank fuck.

Now he needed a hot shower, something to eat and a cold beer. Not necessarily in that order. He swung the door wide on the small fridge on his makeshift bench and decided he'd start with the beer.

He'd had a tough time staying focused today and it wasn't like him. He kept thinking about Marina. About how she'd felt last night, how she'd sounded, how she'd taken him to her room, no questions asked, and then how she'd taken *him*. She should have told him to get lost, instead she'd blown his mind.

He grasped his sweaty t-shirt at the back of his neck and tugged it off, letting it drop to the floor in a cloud of white dust. He leaned back against the bench, tipped back his head to take a gulp of ice-cold beer and froze.

"Marina," he breathed.

Jesus, did he summon her with his dirty thoughts?

"Hey. Your door was open."

Yeah. He always kept the house wide open, especially when he was creating a shit ton of mess.

Even framed by the fading light in the doorway he could tell she was wearing another pair of those stretchy pants he'd do almost anything to see from behind. He bet they hugged the curves of her ass to perfection.

"You left something at my place," she added, hefting the axe she held in her hand and leaning it against a wall.

"Careful," he warned. "It's sharp."

Damn. He'd forgotten all about his axe after her ex had shown up. The first guy she'd kissed, the first one she'd been with. The one she'd had a child with.

Roarke had hated him on sight. He was everything he wasn't—polished and sophisticated with his clean, manicured nails and his hundred dollar hair cut. Not to mention the fancy ride he'd had parked at the curb.

He might make a fortune flipping houses, but he still wouldn't blow over a hundred grand on a car. He looked down at his hands covered in a layer of drywall dust. Probably some grout and who knew what else. He couldn't remember the last time his fingernails had been that clean. Shit. Maybe never.

When he glanced back up she was looking at his chest and it probably wasn't to appreciate his pecs. He knew she wondered. Just as he knew she'd never ask.

"Wrong end of a filthy knife," he bit out.

The words fell from him. They should have been hard to say—they always had been before—but they weren't. Not with Marina. He'd given up wondering why.

Her eyes lifted to his. "So they *are* stab wounds."

He shrugged. She'd have had more of an idea of what they were than most, although some of them had been covered over by the surgical scars.

"There's a lot," she added.

"Nineteen."

"God, Roarke."

The number was etched into his consciousness. He'd felt every single one slice their way into his flesh. He dreamed about it, woke up drenched in sweat remembering. Except when those images came at him, they were in agonizing slow motion, not the frenzied fury it'd been in real-time.

"If she'd had better aim and some decent upper body strength, I'd probably be dead."

Her eyes widened. "She?"

He took another swig from the bottle, looked down as he twirled it by the neck between his hands. "Yeah. She stabbed me while I was trying to stop her detonating the bomb strapped to her and her baby."

He'd managed to wrestle the trigger from her, but if he'd let go, even for a fraction of a second, they would have all died, including the baby. The knife might have had a short blade, but it'd still hurt like a motherfucker.

"At the time I thought it was a better alternative than blowing her head off."

The thing was, faced with the identical scenario, he'd still do the same fucking thing. Ignore orders to take the shot and try to be a hero instead. And what had he been left with? Nightmares and regrets. Because he might have saved them that day, but who the hell knew the next day or the next day after that?

He glanced up at Marina. She'd paled, had her hand up over her mouth and he should be kicking his own ass for telling her something like that. That knowledge wasn't for someone like her. It should be for someone like him to keep to his fucking self.

"Sorry," he forced out. "People think those of us who came back are the lucky ones. I'm not so sure about that."

He'd heard it hundreds of times. How lucky he was. To have made it. To be able to come home. For that fucking knife to miss most of his major organs. To live through his wounds and beat the infections. But he'd never felt lucky, not once. Not until Marina looked at him, with that quiet acceptance she had, not until she'd seen him, the real him, but still wanted him anyway.

"Are they part of why you hadn't been with anyone in a long time?" Her voice was soft and eased some of the tension in his shoulders.

"No," he bit out.

It wasn't what they looked like. Seriously, he didn't give a fuck about that.

"The things I've seen, the things I've done, they stripped something out of me. The ability to feel for one. For good."

"No."

He frowned. "You refusing to believe me doesn't change the facts. I'm broken, Marina. I know it. I accept it. You should too."

She tilted her head to the side. "I'll tell you some facts. You feel. Maybe too much and that's your problem. You've shut that part of you down. Like a protective mechanism. Because you care. And you feel."

He shook his head. "My job was to kill people. And I did."

Coldly and with precision. Because that was his job. What he'd been trained for. What had been expected of him.

"Before they killed you. Before they hurt—"

"Dead is still dead."

"Roarke—"

"What are you doing here, Marina?"

He knew. Of course he did. His heart rate had kicked up the moment he saw her. But he wanted to hear her say it, needed her to, even though he wasn't sure he was good company or any kind of company right now. Even if that kind of company involved her flat on her back under him.

"Sam's with her dad tonight so I came to return your axe and…" She bit her lip and walked toward him, stopping between his outstretched legs, almost touching but not quite. She dropped her gaze to his chest—then lower—and damn if his stomach muscles didn't tighten at the look in her eyes. "I thought I could practice my blow job skills."

Roarke choked on the mouthful of beer he'd just taken. He coughed, wiped at his mouth with the back of his hand.

"I mean, I'm not great at it, so don't get your hopes up or anything, but I want to know what you taste like, how you feel in my mouth, what—"

He reached out and placed a hand across her mouth before the images in his head caused him to combust where he stood.

"Is this your version of foreplay?" he growled.

Her felt her lips move against his palm. She'd smiled. He saw it in her eyes.

She batted his arm aside. Yep. Smiling.

"Is it working?"

And who the fuck had given her the idea she wasn't great at it? Yeah, no way he wanted to know that, but he had a pretty good idea. Fucker. God, she deserved... He didn't know what, but it was more than him, more than what he had.

He tossed the empty beer bottle into the wheelie bin he hadn't taken outside yet, satisfied when it broke with a loud smash.

His touch had left a white streak on her cheek. She bit her lip when he lifted a finger to brush it off and just transferred more to her smooth, creamy skin. He looked down at his dusty boots and plaster-spattered pants. There was even drywall dust in the hairs on his arms.

"I'm filthy."

She gave him a look so hot he felt the heat in his cheeks. "That's, um...what I was sort of counting on."

He groaned. "You can't say things like that to me, Marina."

She laughed. "I just did."

He brushed some of the dust off his chest. "I have to shower."

"Then hurry."

Roarke pushed himself away from the bench, already mapping out in his mind how he could have the fastest shower in recorded history.

"Wait." She frowned. "No crutches?"

"Nope." And it hadn't been soon enough for him.

"I saw the doctor this morning. She said no crutches, no physio, no follow-up." He motioned to the fridge. "Help yourself to a beer if you want."

He'd be glad if he never saw another pair of crutches again. He had his pants undone before he got to the bedroom. He toed off his boots and socks and left them by the bedroom door so that he wouldn't track the dust into his room. Or not much anyway.

It only took a few minutes to soap up and wash the grime out of his hair, towel off most of the water and grab a pair of sweats to yank on. Christ, anyone would think he was worried she'd change her mind.

When he came out of the bathroom, she was in his room, kneeling on the floor next to...

Shit.

"Roarke, these are incredible." She held up one of the more complicated 3-D stars. "And you keep them in an old..." she tilted her head to the side to read the print, "tile box?"

He shrugged. What else would he do with them? He'd taught himself Origami to help pass the time. When he was too exhausted to run, too tired to work on the house, too jacked up to sleep. The level of detail, precision and discipline appealed to him. He'd cycled through a bunch of designs from abstract to animals, even fucking flowers. He'd even started making his own designs. Once he filled up the box, he tossed them and started over.

When she straightened he had a clear view of her ass in those snug pants for a split second and yeah, it was just as spectacular as he'd imagined.

She took a plain black band off her wrist, lifted her arms and put her hair up in a ponytail with a few quick twists. Her gaze was already heated, a flush to her cheeks.

The blood roared in his ears, anticipation a raging inferno inside him. Aw, shit. She meant business.

"I want to do it from when you're still soft," she murmured.

He pushed out a rough laugh. Was she kidding?

"Too late." That ship had sailed the minute he'd laid eyes on her.

He sat down in the only seating he had in the room, an old wooden kitchen chair he used to put his boots on. It wasn't exactly comfortable, but in a few minutes he didn't think he'd give a shit.

She kept her eyes on his as she knelt between his legs, tucked her fingers in the waistband of his sweats and tugged. He lifted his hips and eased them down enough so that his dick sprang free.

"You have no idea how beautiful you are," she whispered.

Yeah. Right. He would have scoffed except she curled her hand around him in that exact moment. All he could do was suck in a breath. Her hand was cool against his hot skin—cool and smooth and so fucking good.

"Are you just going to look at it?" he drawled when she didn't move. And God, he needed her to move.

She licked her lips and his gaze was drawn to her mouth and those full, wet lips.

"I'm trying to decide."

She trailed her fingertips up his length then cupped him in her palm for a single, slow, firm stroke.

"On?" he forced out. It was all he could do not to

wrap his hand around hers, tightening her grip and thrusting up into her hand.

"Well, I could go slow and gentle. Start with some licks and build up from there, maybe just suck the head. Or I could just say what the hell and try to stuff as much as I could in my mouth all at once, as far as I could take you."

Christ.

He groaned. "You're killing me here, Marina."

She bent to him, hesitated. His leg flexed in anticipation, the move so slight she might not have seen it.

A soft, slow lick? Or a full-mouth, nothing-held-back engulf and suck?

"*Marina.*"

Her eyes lifted to his. "In case there's any confusion, I want you to come in my mouth."

Fuck.

She bent close to him, sighed. He flinched at the wash of her breath over him.

"And afterward?" she breathed. "I want you to come inside me."

"Marina," he forced out. "I'm not a sex machine, you know."

She sighed again, her hand tightening around him. "You could be. You totally could be."

* * * * *

Marina woke to heat against her back, an inferno raging inside her. It was a heat that could only be generated by a male body. A solid, unyielding male body. She lay on her side, Roarke pressed against her—close—his hot breath against her skin, his hardness firm against her ass.

She shivered when his mouth closed over the curve of her shoulder, moved up her neck to just under her ear, licking and sucking the sensitive skin there.

"This is your morning wake-up call," he murmured.

Oh, God, she'd stayed the night. She hadn't meant to, but he'd shown her how agile he could be without having to baby his leg and she'd been wiped out.

She had work, so she really needed to get going.

"If—if you kiss my neck, I'm not responsible for what happens next."

"Yeah?" he murmured, rubbing his beard against her neck before closing his teeth over the line of muscle there. He nibbled and kissed and used his teeth to score her skin, over and over. "Then leave it to me."

She gasped when a hard, rough hand cupped her breast, molded her shape, and again when his fingers rolled a nipple between them.

"Roarke, God, I—"

His hand slid down over her stomach until his fingers eased between her legs. And then they were there, right there, rubbing against her clit until her hips began jerking back against him.

It was good, great, God...amazing, but she needed more—more pressure, more depth, just...*more*.

"Roarke," she whimpered.

"I'm here."

A low groan tore from her when he slid two fingers deep. She shuddered, arched back against him and closed her eyes as he thrust them in and out, slow, shallow, and damn, still not enough. The best she could do was rock into his hand, against his fingers as they plowed into her in a steady, mind-destroying rhythm.

She made to turn around. She wanted to look at him, touch him, offer herself to him, tell him he could do anything to her so that he'd stop teasing, but he held her in place with an arm across her body.

"*Roarke*," she sobbed.

"Shhhh. I only wanted to make sure you were ready."

Ready? She was going to die she was so ready.

Her heart slammed against her chest when he withdrew his fingers and she heard the familiar crinkle. The tremble started in her legs and spread until every part of her shook in anticipation. Her throat went chalk dry when his hand brushed the curves of her ass with his movements. Because she knew what he was doing, what was coming. And that it was going to be her. And soon.

She felt the heat and wetness between her legs when he adjusted his position behind her, tried to take a steadying breath, but it was no use. She couldn't get enough air.

"I want to fuck you," he breathed at her ear.

Oh God.

"Just like this."

And then she could barely think as he lifted her thigh over his and slid into her from behind, no hesitation, just delicious expert precision.

She gasped as he filled her, thick and iron hard, the angle driving him against some part of her that almost made her come right then.

Forceful. Gentle. It seemed impossible to be both, but he was. Every. Time.

She wanted to take a second to get used to him, but his fingers dug softly into her hip, holding her in place as he began to move.

Hard heat speared through her, out from where they were joined, his thrusts deep and slow. The hair-roughened skin of his thighs against the backs of hers created a friction that caused a tingling all the way down her legs to her toes. Or it could have been his thick length, stretching her wide with each pump.

That hand slid down over her tummy again, his fingers spread wide over the soft curve, anchoring her against him. She couldn't move, couldn't thrust the way she wanted, the way she needed. All she could do was accept his depth and the pace he set.

Her clit ached, throbbed. Before she was aware of what she was doing, her hand was between her legs. She rubbed against herself, right where it stung, gasping at the sensation of her own fingers. It still wasn't enough.

"Let me."

Roarke brushed her hand aside and she whimpered. Until he replaced her fingers with his own. He began flicking back and forth against her clit, fast, frenzied movements, all while he maintained the relentless, unyielding rhythm. God, she could almost imagine it was his tongue between her legs.

Marina arched back against him as he nibbled and sucked and licked at the skin of her neck. She shivered at the sensation of his hot breath against her, sawing in and out of his heavy chest in time to the force of his thrusts, his talented fingers, the sound a roar in her ear.

"I'm..."

She'd been going to say "close" but she never got

the chance. Sensation exploded through her body, curling out from where they were joined until it made her a quivering mass of pleasure—shaking, gasping, blind.

She clutched at his arm, driving his fingers harder against her as she rode out wave after wave of pleasure until it evened out, until she could finally open her eyes.

"Roarke," she choked out because he hadn't stopped moving, hadn't even slowed down. "Please."

His harsh breathing was still a loud roar in her ear and she could feel his thundering heartbeat against her back.

"Sorry," he rasped, his movements stilling.

He hissed when he eased out of her and Marina frowned. He was still thick and hard. She'd felt him. It was almost as if...

"Roarke—"

"I gotta go."

He eased off the bed, made for the bathroom. She sat up, her limbs shaky, but no way was she going to miss an opportunity to look at him, not full view. Her mouth went dry at the sight of hard muscles sliding under the smooth skin of his back and the curves of his firm ass. It was hard to believe she'd ridden that body, had had her hands all over him, been under him.

She bit her lip at the surge of heat, but in an instant it was gone. As he walked into the bathroom and turned for the shower, he was still fully erect.

Marina almost stumbled over her own feet when she got to the bathroom doorway, because holy crap.

Roarke. In the shower. One arm braced on the wall in front of him, his head bowed under the spray and his other hand... God, his other hand was wrapped around himself, jerking in a series of sharp tugs.

Heat surged through her, blooming low in her abdomen and then even lower. The muscles of his upper arm flexed with each movement and her mouth went dry, her heartbeat kicked back up, and the still-sensitive flesh between her legs throbbed.

He grunted when he came, the sound so low she almost missed it over the running water.

Holy. Shit.

Marina released the breath she'd been holding in a long, shaky exhale as he washed himself off, the movements quick and efficient. She'd never watched a guy do that before, hadn't realized how...hot it could be, how intense, how much of a turn-on.

Her breath caught at the sharp punch to her gut when he shut off the water and stepped out of the shower. She'd never, ever get used to the impact of seeing him naked. Nothing hidden, no hint of modesty, just powerful male confidence.

He glanced at her before reaching for his towel and she swallowed against the thickness in her throat because she knew. He'd known she was there, watching him and he'd done it anyway.

"That—that might just be the hottest thing I've ever seen," she managed. "But don't walk away from me to do that ever again. I could have—"

"No."

She frowned. "Why not?"

She really wanted to ask him why he hadn't come, why he hadn't let her help him, pleasure him, but all the old doubts came rushing back at her. Maybe she sucked at this sex-with-the-hot-guy stuff. Maybe she'd sucked at the blow job last night. How would she even know?

He knotted a towel around his waist and turned to her. His face was drawn in tight lines, his gaze dark and intense when it raked over her, lingering on all her girlie parts.

Shit, how could she have forgotten she was naked too?

"What I gave you was a gift, freely given. Just for you."

"But—"

"If I'd come, if you'd reciprocated, it wouldn't have been a gift."

She licked her lips and the look in his eyes caused her breath to catch. "I—I don't understand."

"I've got precious little to give anyone, Marina, but I can at least give you that. It was a gift, okay? From me to you." He shrugged. "No big deal."

Right. She nodded, but not about it not being a big deal. It was huge.

He'd given her pleasure and hadn't taken his own when he could have.

She walked to him and stopped, her steps slow and sure when everything in her felt anything but. This close she could feel the heat coming off his big body from the shower and smell the soap he'd used. A lone drop of water hugged the hard curve of one pec muscle. What she wouldn't give to be brave enough to lean forward and lick it.

Marina sighed. He was hot and clean and from the bulge at the front of his towel, not exactly fully satisfied. She wanted nothing more than to drop to her knees in front of him, yank at the towel and thank him with her mouth.

She bit her lip. God, now she could imagine how he'd taste, how he'd feel against her tongue, how he'd fill her mouth, the sounds he'd make. God, she wanted him inside her again. Right now. Up against the wall, on the vanity, anywhere, didn't matter.

He stiffened when she put her hand on his chest and locked her gaze with his. His jaw clenched, his eyes wary, almost as if he were braced for something.

Everything about him screamed mean and dangerous. The muscles, the stark tattoos, the darkness in the depths of his eyes and God, the scars. He should have scared her. At the very least made her wary. But he never had. She'd known he was different from the first time she'd looked into his eyes.

This man had given up his own pleasure. For her. So, okay, it might have been some screwy logic, but God…it was so damn sweet, so hot, so…

Marina sighed and swallowed back all the words she wanted to say, because she knew he wouldn't want them. Besides, she'd promised him she could do this only-sex thing. She didn't want to break any rules, especially her own.

"You know," she whispered instead, leaning in close, almost smiling when she saw his eyes narrow in warning. "You're the best damn alarm clock I ever had."

CHAPTER EIGHT

Roarke's crew was at his other property today, so he had the radio cranked up, hoping the sound would help him focus. No such luck so far.

He knew it wasn't real, but he'd swear he could still smell her—the scent of her hair, whatever she used on her skin, her sweat after she came. He was working in the master bedroom today, finishing up the framing for the large antique doors he'd sourced. Or trying to. If he closed his eyes, he could almost hear her moans, the way she'd panted when he'd been plowing into her from behind earlier.

He'd been trying to keep his eyes off the bed, from the twisted sheets he hadn't bothered with. He'd found her panties after she'd left, tucked under the edge of the sheet. He'd thrown them in with his dirty clothes, but fuck, it'd been hard not to put them up to his nose, to smell them, her.

He straightened. The solo shower action hadn't done a thing to satisfy him. It didn't help that what kept punching into his head was how she'd looked after she'd watched him jerk off.

Her cheeks had been flushed, her bottom lip red where she'd bitten it, her nipples hard little points he'd wanted to lick and suck. Yeah, she'd been turned on. Big time.

He sighed when yet another news alert came over the radio, bit back his frustration. He'd had it blaring all morning and everything seemed to be on repeat. He was just about to flip to Bluetooth and his playlist when he froze.

"This is a breaking news alert. University Hospital along Randall Road is closed as police respond to a hostage situation that started around 12:30 p.m. today."

Roarke frowned and glanced at his watch. Thirty minutes ago.

"The public is encouraged to stay out of the area as police deal with this standoff. If people have a non-emergency concern requiring care, please seek attention at another medical facility. University Hospital personnel and medics are ready with ambulances to transport those coming to the hospital requiring immediate emergency attention."

He lowered the nail gun to the floor, felt his focus zero in.

"At this time a man is believed to be holding several hospital personnel at gunpoint near the hospital's ER."

Aw, fuck.

Roarke's gut clenched and he felt the familiar rush of adrenaline, welcomed it. Marina was at work. Who the hell knew if she was anywhere near the ER?

"The police will be providing updates as more information becomes available. This is a developing news story so stay tuned. We'll bring you those updates as we have them."

He grabbed his phone. It took a split second for him to decide not to call her. A ringing phone could be a distraction in a heightened situation, a dangerous distraction.

He unclipped his tool belt and let it drop with a loud thud. He grabbed the keys to his truck, headed to the front door, already mapping out the fastest route to the hospital in his head.

It was stupid, he knew it was. He didn't even know what the hell he was going to do, but he sure as fuck wasn't going to sit around here with his finger up his ass waiting for another news report. Not when Marina could be in danger.

There'd been no additional information on the radio by the time Roarke made it to the hospital. Three cop cars were parked out front of the hospital and a SWAT van pulled up just as he cruised past. They hadn't closed off any roads yet, so he pulled into a side street and took the first open spot. It wasn't really a park, but what the fuck?

He walked toward the back of the buildings. Shit, the place was huge. He scanned the crowd of people who came running out of a side door. None were Marina, but he recognized one of the nurses. The one who'd thrown a fit when he'd taken out his own IV.

Roarke grabbed her arm as she hurried past him. "Where's Marina?" he bit out.

She looked at him in confusion. "I…"

"*Marina*. Where is she?"

"She's… ER today. I think. I didn't see her. Oh, God…"

His gut tightened along with his hold on her arm.

"Did you see the intruder?"

"Just a glimpse. I remember you. You were—"

"One man?"

The news said one, but the information might not

be accurate.

She nodded. "What—"

"Are you sure?" Roarke pushed.

"Yes."

"He's armed?"

"Yes. He—"

"What type of weapon?"

"I—I don't know. A gun, I don't know what type. I—"

"Demeanor?"

She frowned. "Demeanor?"

Roarke bit back the impatience. "Did he seem agitated? Calm? Angry? Confused?"

"Ah...he—he seemed upset, he was yelling. I think he said something about the hospital hiding something from him."

Shit. Possibly mentally unstable.

"Where is he now?"

"He came in through emergency. I was coming back from break when I caught sight of him. I think—I think he was heading toward the PACU."

"The what?"

"PACU. The post-anesthesia care unit. You—you were there when you came out of the OR."

"How do I get there from here?" He motioned to the door she'd just come out of. "If I go through that door?"

She shook her head. "It's complicated. I..."

"Focus. I need clear, directional instructions. The fastest route."

"Okay, um, through the doors, straight down the corridor until you get to the very end. Take a left. There'll be a set of elevators. Go up to the first floor. Go right, through a set of double doors. To another bank of elevators. Go back down a floor. When you come out you should be right there. You'll see the signs…"

Roarke let her go and turned toward the door, already creating a virtual map in his mind.

"Wait. You can't…"

He ignored her, rushed for the door, dodging the people still filing out. He bypassed the elevator and took the stairs, two at a time, ignoring the twinge in his leg, accepting that he'd probably pay for it later. He tried a light jog down the empty corridor, favoring his left leg as much as possible and took the stairs again back down.

When he cracked open the door to the floor he winced.

"*Where is she? Where have you hidden her?*"

The shout was loud, panicked. Demeanor definitely not calm or rational.

"Sir, please…"

"*Shut up.* Stop with the lies."

Shit.

Roarke swallowed back the bitter taste in his mouth. That'd been Marina's voice. He'd hoped like fuck she'd made it out, that she was somewhere else, but he'd had a sinking feeling since he'd heard the news report. His instincts had never let him down. Not once. He was alive because he'd learned to listen to them.

He slipped into the corridor and eased into the first treatment room. He grabbed the hospital gown at the foot of the bed, toed off his boots and socks and yanked off his work pants. He thrust his arms through the gown and hoped like hell he could pass for a patient.

"Tell me where she is. *Now*. I know you're keeping her here."

"I swear to you she's not here. She—she left."

Marina's voice trailed off and Roarke took a deep breath. He stepped back out into the corridor, keeping close to the wall. When he reached the corner, he got his first good look at the threat.

Middle-aged man. Average build. Unkempt. The way he held the gun told Roarke he hadn't had any specialized training. Possibly mentally unstable. And fuck…he stood with his gun pointed directly at Marina.

She was pale, standing out in front of a group of hospital staff and patients, cowering behind her. She opened her mouth when she saw him. He gave a slight shake of his head, hoping like hell she would know he didn't want her to draw any attention to him.

Fear. He thought he knew what it was, that he'd lived with it long enough, learned to conquer it on a daily basis. He'd had no fucking clue before this. Even as a SEAL he'd never felt this type of fear before. He'd put himself in danger all the time. Every fucking day. Risk was part of what he'd done, what he'd signed up for. He might have even got off on the adrenaline rush of it in the beginning.

But this? The churning, twisting cold that felt like shards of glass in his veins? He'd never felt anything like it before because right now Marina was directly in the line of fire, putting herself between the assailant and the others. Protective. Calm. Brave. And un-fucking-acceptable.

He stepped forward. It was go time.

The man's eyes snapped to him, but he kept the gun steady on Marina.

"Get over there." He motioned with the weapon to the group, just as Roarke had anticipated.

Roarke lifted his hands away from his body, continued to take easy, slow steps until he stood in front of her, blocking her from the guy's view, until the gun pointed directly at his own chest.

"It's cool, man," Roarke murmured.

Now that he had his attention, Roarke inched to the right. The gun wavered, but followed his movement.

Thank fuck.

"Hey, don't move," he demanded.

Roarke spread his arms wide out in front of him. "Take it easy, man," he murmured, keeping his voice low and even, moving another few inches.

"I said don't move."

Roarke kept his movements slow, but kept moving to the right and forward until he was sure Marina was clear behind him.

"You're scaring everyone, man," Roarke offered. The man's eyes widened as if that had never occurred to him. "All the women, they're scared. What would your wife think about that?"

When the gun lowered, when his eyes shifted from him to the group of nurses, Roarke was ready. And made his move.

He grabbed the gun and stepped into the man. Before he had a chance to react, he'd jerked it to the side and out of his hand with the momentum of his movement, ignoring the screams behind him, blocking out everything but what was right in front of him.

The guy's eyes went wide, but it was too late. Roarke had already emptied the clip along with the round in the chamber. And fuck if it hadn't been fully loaded. He tossed the useless weapon on the floor and froze when the guy pulled out a knife.

Roarke ground his back teeth together until his jaw clicked. Anger rose inside of him in a wave, like a red haze over his eyes. A knife. Did it have to be a knife? Couldn't it have been anything other than a Goddamn knife?

Roarke charged him before he had a chance to get into an offensive position. He grabbed the hand that held the knife. And twisted. Hard.

The snap of bone was loud. It was swallowed up by the scream of pain that quickly followed.

"I'm sorry, man," Roarke grunted. "But no one points a gun at anyone I consider mine and no one—and I mean *no one*—pulls a fucking knife on me. Not ever again."

He kicked the guy's legs out from under him. Roarke should have felt bad when he hit the ground hard, cradling his hand, but he didn't. He just hoped like hell he didn't have any more weapons.

Roarke took several deep breaths, tried to get the adrenaline rush under control. He reached for the cold, the calm, the controlled, but he couldn't get a handle on it. The rage continued to roll through him, the fear almost a living thing inside him he couldn't harness.

He held the knife out away from his side when he heard the rumble of boots behind him.

"*Freeze.*"

He lifted his arms up and away from his body. He didn't feel like getting shot, not today. He glanced over at Marina. Even though she had her hands over her mouth, he could see she was pale. Her eyes were wide and her gaze when it met his was glazed. Probably shock.

Didn't matter. Nothing did. Because she was safe.

And then all hell broke loose.

KAILY HART

CHAPTER NINE

Roarke was standing in the shower, head bowed under the water, both hands braced against the tile in front of him. He was all hard muscles and stark ink and her already fast pulse kicked up a notch.

"*Leave.*"

The rough word grated over her already raw nerve endings. Guttural and deep, it held so much animosity Marina almost took a step back, but screw that.

It'd been total chaos at the hospital once the police had arrived. And they hadn't listened to her, hadn't taken any notice of her screaming or her pleading, her attempts to explain. They'd taken Roarke into custody with the other man and dragged him away. And they'd questioned her and the others for what seemed like hours. After they'd all given their statements they'd been free to go, but even though she knew Roarke had been released, he'd ignored all her calls and texts.

"Get the fuck out of here, Marina. *Now.*"

She wanted… God, she didn't know what she

wanted. To thank him, to make sure he wasn't hurt, to... She clenched her hands into fists. She wanted, *needed* him to reassure her dammit, that he was okay, that she was okay, to hold her because she felt as if she was going to break into a million tiny pieces any minute.

"Not going to happen," she managed.

He shut off the water with a violent twist and stepped out of the shower, all wet, smooth skin, flexing muscles and aggressive male.

"You fucking asked for it then."

She gasped when he walked right to her—eyes narrowed—in a handful of fast, easy strides. He backed her into the wall, placed his hands flat on each either side of her head and leaned down until his eyes were level with hers.

Marina was locked into place by his nearness, his heat, caged in his stance. She frowned. Why the hell was he so angry? His dark gaze was feral. Yeah, angry didn't even scratch the surface.

"You don't ever do anything like that again," he forced out. "Do you hear me?"

Hear him? She could feel his words against her face.

"Roarke," she choked out. "I—"

"Jesus fucking Christ, Marina, he pointed a gun at you. Right at you."

Yeah, she'd been there.

"Roarke—"

"That is unacceptable. Do you understand? You do not step in front of someone with a fucking gun."

"You did," she shot back, because she'd never forget seeing that gun pointed at *him*, how he'd made himself a target, so calmly, as if it were nothing.

"Yeah. It's what I'm trained for. I broke that man's hand, Marina. With purpose and precision because I could and it was the most efficient way to take control of the situation."

"I know," she whispered.

"Because I'm a trained killer."

"Roarke—"

"Enough." He pushed himself off the wall and stepped back. "You need to leave. *Go.*"

"Will you," she choked out. "Just for one minute, shut up and hold me?"

His eyes narrowed into dangerous slits. "Hold you? You want comfort?" He spread his arms out wide, glanced down at his own body before raking her with a searing glance that enveloped her from head to foot in hot, dirty heat. "This is how I can comfort you."

Oh, God. The sound of her own heartbeat roared in her ears. He was hard, full and thick.

"If you wanna fuck," he added, "I'm up for it, but what I have in me right now is hard, fast, angry sex. You up for *that*?"

She should have been intimidated by his size, his nakedness, his aggression, but she wasn't—at all—because she saw through his bullshit for what it was.

"Stop it," she snapped.

"Stop what?"

"Being nasty."

He snorted. "You've known me long enough to know 'being nasty' is part of my make up."

"No. You use it to push people away."

"So?"

"Just like you're doing right now."

"Again... So?"

So it didn't work on her, not really, although that didn't mean it still didn't hurt.

"I really want to tell you to go to hell right now," she managed.

He tilted his head back, all arrogant male challenge. "Then why don't you? I sure as fuck deserve it."

Yeah.

"Because that's what you expect, what you want. So I'll just take the hard, fast, angry sex instead."

His brows shot down over his eyes. "Marina—"

"But I'll do what I wanted to do at the hospital first—before everything went sideways—and you'll damn well let me."

She stepped forward before he could figure out what she was going to do, wrapped her arms around his waist, laid her cheek against his chest, let her eyes drift shut and held on. Tight.

There was no softness on his big body. None. She'd never get used to how hard he was, how unyielding. He kept his hands by his sides, but she didn't care. She needed to feel his warmth, be close to him, reassure herself that he was okay, even if he was being an asshole.

"I'm fine, Roarke," she forced out, her voice muffled against his chest. "Because you made sure of it."

One of his hands clenched in the back of her hair. He shuddered against her. She heard him swallow.

"I blame you, Marina. I blame you for all of it."

His words were barely audible, thick and hoarse.

She pulled back so that she could look into his face. "Blame me for what?"

"I blame you for making me scared for you, I

blame you for making me feel blind, sheer terror for the first time in my life and I blame you for—Goddamn it, Marina," he forced out. "I blame you for making me *feel* again."

The punch to her gut was fast, sharp. "Oh, Roarke."

He walked her back a step until she was against the wall again. "And you were supposed to say no to the hard, fast, angry sex."

How could she? He was hurting, whether he'd ever admit it or not.

He reached over to a drawer in the vanity and yanked it open. "Hold this," he bit out.

Marina took the condom packet with a trembling hand. He kept his gaze locked to hers as he slipped rough hands under the waistband of her scrubs and yanked them down, taking her panties with them.

Heat surged through her, and she shivered at the brush of his fingers against naked skin. He crouched, pushing the pants all the way to her ankles. And then he stilled. And just looked at her. There.

His nostrils flared. God, he was smelling her. She bit her lip as he leaned forward, the flesh between her legs already hot, getting wetter by the second.

She gasped and then moaned when he put his mouth between her legs in a bold, open-mouthed kiss. He sucked her clit into his mouth and ate at her, hard and frenzied, the suckling sounds almost as mind-destroying as the broad flat of his tongue against her. There. Right there. Where she needed it. So bad.

She shifted her legs as far apart as she could, threaded her fingers through his hair and drove her hips against that relentless tongue, matching his rhythm as she fought for breath. The rasp of his beard against the sensitive skin of her thighs—and higher, between her legs—seared her from head to foot and she shook at the intensity of it.

"Roarke," she whimpered when he stood without warning. God, she'd been a split second, less, away from exploding against his mouth.

"Put it on me."

The words were low and rough and it took a moment for his words to register. The flesh between her legs throbbed, stung, almost as if it knew what was coming.

While he watched her tear open the packet, he slid a rough hand between her legs and without any hesitation he eased a hard finger into her. He gave her no time to get used to it, to him, before he began pumping in and out.

"Roarke," she panted, finding it almost impossible to keep her eyes open. "I can't…"

God, her fingers wouldn't work. She bit her lip, reached down, managed to get the rubber onto the head of his cock. Just as she went to roll it down, he added a second finger, filling her, stretching her.

"Please," she begged.

"I need you close before I get inside you, Marina. I'm going to last no fucking time at all."

Her hand engulfed him and he hissed at the contact. As soon as she'd rolled it down as far as she could, he eased his fingers from her and moved between her legs, pushing himself between her folds.

And then he surged into her in one sure stroke. She clutched for his shoulders when he grasped her hips, lifted and pinned her against the wall.

She threw her head back, closed her eyes,

swamped with sensation, filled and stretched, trapped by his big, heavy, heaving body.

When he didn't move, she opened her eyes with an effort.

A pulse flexed at his temple, his dark eyes glazed with pleasure.

"Okay?" he rasped.

"Oh, God. *Yes.*"

"Then hold on."

She wrapped her legs around his hips, clasped her arms around his massive shoulders.

His fingers clenched into the soft flesh of her hips and he began to move. Thick and long he surged into her, once, twice, a third time before he froze, groaned into her neck.

"I'm—"

She been going to say "coming", but didn't get the word out, couldn't. Sensation, sharp and powerful, exploded through her, blinding and deafening her to everything around her, until the only thing she was aware of was Roarke, his ragged breathing at her neck, his guttural grunts of pleasure as he thrust through his own orgasm, drawing out her own.

"Okay?"

This time all she could do was nod.

She sucked in a breath when he eased from her body, steadying her until she stood. Her heart was racing, her body trembling and her legs, they were still shaking.

God, he hadn't been messing around when he'd said hard and fast. She felt hot color flood her cheeks when she looked down. She still had her top on.

Before he could step away from her, she put both hands on his cheeks, brought him down to her.

His gaze might already be shuttered, emotions hidden, locked down, but the remnants of pleasure—pleasure he'd gotten from her—was still stamped on his features. His eyes were darker than usual, cheeks flushed, the lines beside his mouth less defined. His features were bold and strong and his mouth... God, those full lips and what they could do to her, what they had done to her.

He frowned. "What are you doing?"

"Taking a good, long look," she said, her voice soft because that's as much as she could manage. "You know, in case I never see you again."

"Marina—"

"It's okay. I knew what this was."

He scowled. "Oh, really? And what's that?"

He was annoyed. Good.

She cleared her throat, fought against the churning emotion she didn't have a handle on, not yet. "I caught you off guard."

"No one catches me off guard," he shot back.

Right.

"You let me in for a split second, Roarke—each and every time—but I always knew there was a chance it wouldn't be any longer than that."

* * * * *

God, who could have known? Fast, angry sex with Marina was just as unsatisfying as solo shower sex. Almost.

Roarke scrubbed a hand down over his face. She'd been through a traumatic experience and what had he done? He'd yelled at her for fuck's sake. She'd been sheet white and he'd yelled at her. Shit, he couldn't remember the last time he'd lost control enough to raise his voice. And then he'd fucked her senseless up against his bathroom wall.

Not his best moment.

He knew what he should have done. He should have grabbed her and held on and not let go. Except there were no do-overs.

Damn. He'd let her walk. He'd needed time, time to realize she was really safe, time to get his fucking head together, time to figure out how he was going to undo all of it because right this moment he still had no clue.

Yeah, he'd made a mess of pretty much everything.

He forced himself to knock before he chickened out and he might have, except the door opened right away.

His stomach clenched. Of course. It figured. Where else would he be?

"Daniels," Jake drawled.

"Evans," Roarke bit out.

Raine gave Jake a warning glare before nudging him aside.

"Roarke, is everything okay?"

"Yeah, sure, I just… Can I come in?"

"Of course."

Roarke shoved his hands in his pockets and waited while Raine closed the door.

She was frowning. "What's going on, Roarke?"

"I—I have something I need to say, something to tell you."

Raine glanced at Jake and then back to him. "Okay."

Her voice was wary. He didn't blame her. He'd

given her nothing but a tough time for a long time now.

"I'll leave you guys to it then," Jake murmured, giving him a hard look. It was a warning, plain and simple, and Roarke got it loud and clear. He wouldn't have expected anything less from him because he knew without a doubt Jake would always put Raine first, that she was his priority no matter what.

"No," Roarke forced out. "Stay. You should hear this too."

It was right. Fair. God, he owed Jake more than he could ever express, not that he'd ever tried, but before today he might not have realized just how much.

"God, spit it out, Roarke," Raine demanded. "You're scaring me."

Yeah, he was scaring himself right now.

He walked to Raine and put his hands on her shoulders, tried to ignore the churn in his gut. He looked her square in the eye because he wanted her to know he was dead serious, that he meant every word.

"Roarke," she warned.

"I was wrong and I'm sorry."

There. He'd said it. He might have gotten it out, but his gut was still twisted in fucking knots.

She was still frowning. "About what?"

Yeah, they both knew he probably had a fuck load to apologize for.

"The whole situation with Lambert. I played it all wrong." He swallowed back the thickness in his throat. "I'm sorry, Raine."

God, this was way harder than he imagined. In fact, it sucked.

"I know you did what you thought was right. That you were just trying to protect me."

Just like Raine. He knew she understood, that she'd always forgiven him for anything. Well, he wouldn't let himself off the hook that easily, even if his intentions had been good.

"No, I kept something from you when I shouldn't have. I thought keeping the fact that Lambert was still stalking you was protecting you. It wasn't. I put you in danger because of it. Christ, I knew he was dangerous and I arrogantly assumed I could run interference, that eventually he'd lose interest. I was one hundred percent wrong."

He glanced over to Jake. "And if I was in your shoes? I would have done the exact same thing you did. I know that now. I never would have let a threat go on indefinitely. Never. I rode your ass hard about it and I apologize."

Jake frowned. "Well, shit."

"Roarke," Raine sighed and stepped into him. He closed his arms around her, held her against him.

"Also?" he murmured against her hair.

She pulled back. "Yes?"

He inclined his head toward Jake, knew he'd hear him. "I do like him."

The truth was Roarke respected the hell out of him. Always had.

She smiled. "I know."

Jake held out his hand when Roarke turned to go. "I like this side of you."

Roarke put his hand against Jake's, clasped hard, nodded at what was offered, given.

"And what side would that be?" he muttered.

Jake's mouth kicked up at one corner. "The groveling side."

"Yeah?" He swallowed, because this was nothing

compared to what he still needed to do. "This was just the warm up."

Christ, he felt as if he was on some twelve-step program for recovering assholes.

CHAPTER TEN

Roarke stopped in front of his second door of the night. He felt choked up, almost as if he were drowning. And maybe he was. The stakes were high. They were fucking everything.

He didn't know what he was going to say, but he knocked anyway, because if he stood waiting around until he figured it out, he'd be here all night.

He let out a rough breath when the kid opened the door.

She smiled. "Hey."

God, he wondered if he'd ever get used to how much she looked like Marina.

"Hey," he managed.

"My Dad asked me about you," she said.

Roarke frowned. "He did?"

Yeah, he just bet he did.

"Yep. I told him to mind his own business and if he wanted to know anything he should ask Mommy."

Ouch.

"Ah…"

"Are you here to see Mommy?"

"Yeah, but..."

He knelt so that he was eye-to-eye with her. He felt the twinge in his hip and ignored it.

"I screwed up with her, kid. I hurt her, even when I swore to myself I wouldn't. So I came to apologize. I'm going to try and fix it."

"You can."

Her gaze was clear and steady and so like Marina it caused a pain to bloom in the middle of his chest.

"I'll try, but regardless of what happens, you and I, we're solid, yeah?"

He smiled, even though his insides felt as if glass shards were twisting around in there.

He held his clenched fist up and she met it with her own. "Solid," she murmured. "Will you still teach me how to do Origami?"

He couldn't make a promise he didn't know he could keep.

"I'm not sure. It'll be up to your mom. But even if she says no, that's cool, right? Because she's...everything."

Roarke cringed. He could barely string words together, nothing coherent anyway. How the fuck he was going to be able to talk to Marina, try to make her understand, be able to make up for all the shit he'd done? He still didn't know what to do or what to say.

The kid nodded and he knew she got it. Instinctively. Somehow.

"Okay, kid. Wish me luck?"

She tilted her head to the side. "You know my real name is Sam, right?"

"I know, but to me you'll always be 'kid'. Is that okay?"

"Okay." She nodded. "Sort of like Melissa's dad when he calls her Cuddle Bear? It's an endeard…ment."

"Ah…" Roarke almost choked against the thickness in his throat. "Yeah, sure."

She frowned. "But what's going to happen if I get a little baby brother or sister? If you call them 'kid' too, won't that be confusing?"

Roarke coughed. Baby? What the hell? Who said anything about a baby? Christ, he didn't think in those terms, never had. That was in a future he'd never dared to imagine in relation to himself.

Maybe the kid knew more about what was going on than he thought. "Ah, that's a long way off, kid." If ever. "Besides, that would be, you know, up to your mom."

Shit.

A baby? Him? He wouldn't know what to do with a baby. He didn't even know what to do with a nine year old.

Besides, first he had to convince a grown woman to take a chance on him. Again. That's even if she'd speak to him.

"Look, I messed up bad with your mom. Really bad. So bad I'm not sure I can undo it."

She patted his arm and gave him a solemn look. "As long as you try your best, that's all you can do. But I know you can fix it."

Her absolute faith slayed him because he didn't think anyone had ever had that level of confidence in him before. Ever. That level of responsibility? Yeah, it scared the hell out of him.

Roarke looked up to see Marina standing just inside the doorway.

"Marina…"

Shit, she'd heard everything he said.

"Sam, what have I told you about opening the door by yourself?"

Yeah, she might have heard what he said, but her face said she wasn't going to make this easy for him.

"I saw that it was Roarke. You had a sleepover with him so he's not a stranger. Right?"

Hot color flooded her cheeks and she bit her lip. Her gaze darted to him before going back to Sam. "Why don't you go in and brush your teeth? Get ready for bed?"

Once she was gone Marina turned to him. "What are you doing here?"

She'd changed out of the scrubs and into a pair of those stretchy pants and a loose t-shirt. And she was still pale.

He swallowed back the huge fucking lump in his throat.

"I'm sorry, Marina." His voice when it came out sounded rusty.

"For what exactly?"

Yeah, not impressed. Did he blame her?

God, she was so beautiful and he'd never told her. Not once. She should have been telling him to fuck off. It's what he deserved. But she didn't. She waited. For what? But he knew. She was waiting for him to man the fuck up and that meant he still had a chance.

"I feel as if I can't fucking breathe right now."

"It's probably the ribs."

"No." He forced out a strangled laugh. "It's you. You did something to me."

Her eyes widened. "*I* did?"

"Yeah."

"The first time you touched me I felt…something. I might not have known what the fuck it was, but I knew it wasn't anything I'd felt before. I also knew it wasn't anything I wanted. At least, that's what I thought. And I can't undo it. I don't even want to anymore."

"Roarke—"

"Do you see that?"

He held his hand out in front of her. It shook. No surprise there.

"No one has ever made my hands shake before. No one. Until you. And I've never felt real fear before today either. I've been scared. Being a SEAL…"

He shook his head. "Yeah, being scared was healthy. It came with the territory, but I will *never*," he forced out, "for as long as I live, forget seeing that gun pointed at you. I think it made me lose my fucking mind for awhile."

He paused when his voice threatened to give out. "Somehow, somewhere along the line you became the most important person in my life and I have no idea how to tell you that. I still don't."

She let out a shaky breath. "I think you just did."

"I'm no good at this shit anymore, Marina. I don't think I ever was."

"Do you trust me, Roarke?"

He looked at her then, her gaze was steady on his and open, so fucking open.

"Trust you?" he choked out. "Don't you know I wouldn't be here if I didn't?"

"Then just tell me what you feel, what you're thinking, right this very minute."

He was silent for a heartbeat, two.

"Right this minute?" He forced out a sound that

could have been a laugh, but came out sharp, abrupt instead. "I can't figure out if I want to kiss the fuck out of you or run as far away from you as I can."

There. She'd asked.

"Well, if it was my choice?" The side of her mouth lifted in a half smile that did nothing to calm the twisting and churning in his gut. "I know which one I'd pick."

Just like that. No more questions, no hesitation. Just trust. What he'd done to deserve that from her, he'll never know. At this point, he'd fucking take it, take anything.

"For a long time it's felt as if everything inside me was frozen. After I came back, I didn't know how to defrost myself. But you've done that, Marina and dammit, I can't freeze again, even if I wanted to." He shook his head. "You scare the hell out of me because of it."

"I don't mean to," she murmured.

She walked the step into him then. Just as she'd done earlier, she wrapped her arms around his waist, rested her head against his chest. This time he wouldn't just stand there like a jerk. He wrapped his arms around her, as tight as he dared and held her against him. God, she felt so small, so soft against him. And this time he'd say what he should have said.

"I'm sorry I yelled at you."

Her arms tightened around him.

"And I'm sorry for the...wall thing. Well, maybe not that exactly, just for everything that went down before and after."

She lifted her head. Her cheeks were flushed, her gaze hot and memories surged through him, hot, explicit memories that had his body hardening in an instant.

"I didn't mind the wall thing."

Oh. Man.

"I might have spewed all that 'just sex' bullshit, Marina, but it's not the sex. I—" He broke off, rubbed a rough hand over his face. "Fuck, who am I kidding? It was fucking totally the sex. At first. But now it's just you. You break me down, Marina, and then you break me apart. Until I have no choice."

"No choice for what?"

He swallowed. "No choice but to let you in. I don't have the right words. I don't— I can't—"

"Love isn't what you say, Roarke," Marina cut in. "It's about what you do. You've shown me how you feel, whether you wanted to or not, whether you knew it or not. And that's all I need. For you to keep showing me."

"I don't know what I did to deserve you, but I thank God for it."

Marina looked down and away from him and his gut clenched.

"What about Sam?" Her voice was low and quiet.

He frowned. "What about her?"

"She's my priority, Roarke."

He wouldn't have expected anything else. He used a finger under her chin so that she'd have to look at him.

"She's yours," he breathed.

Marina frowned. "What—"

"I'm all in here, Marina. I know next to nothing about kids, but she's part of you, so I consider it a package deal. So that means she's my priority too. Both of you. Whatever I have, whatever I'm capable of, is yours. And hers. Now. And always. Deal?"

"Deal." Her own hand when she held it out wasn't exactly steady. "Should we shake on it?"

He felt some of the heaviness lift from him for the first time in a long time. He swiped his thumb across her lower lip.

"Oh, I have a much better way to seal the deal than that."

EPILOGUE

Three Months Later

Marina smiled at the sight he made—muscles straining his t-shirt, tattoos down both arms to his wrists, the tough guy attitude he projected without even trying—carrying Sam's half-eaten, mostly melted blue raspberry snow cone.

She only had to look at him to get breathless, to have her heartbeat kick up, for the churning in her stomach to start. But not just because of what he looked like. Maybe despite it, because underneath all that hot, sexy toughness was a protective streak a mile wide, a core of goodness, of integrity, that was damn rare, and a man who'd risked his own life—no hesitation, no questions asked—for *her*.

He took a sip when he sat down next to her and screwed up his face.

"Christ, how does she eat this?"

"Careful." Marina laughed. "You'll get a blue tongue."

"Yeah?" In an instant his eyes went dark and dirty and dangerous. "Then later you'll get a blue—"

"*Stop.*"

Marina looked around to make sure no one had heard him and he smiled—a flash of white, even teeth that went straight to his eyes. A real smile. Natural and easy. Just for her. God, she'd never get tired of seeing that.

When she turned back to the game, her own smiled died and everything in her went still because Sam was putting on her batting helmet.

"What did you say to him?" she whispered.

Roarke had gone down to talk to Sam in the dugout and Marina had seen him chatting to the coach.

"That if he didn't put the kid in the game I'd break both his arms."

He said it so matter-of-factly it took a few seconds for the words to sink in.

"Are you kidding?" she choked.

"Yeah."

"Yeah...what?"

He turned to her then. "That's what I wanted to say, but I restrained myself. For you. And the kid." He shrugged. "I told him she's been practicing really hard and she's earned a shot."

This season Sam had sat on the bench more times than she'd played. Marina had tried a bunch of times to talk to the coach, but he'd always brushed her off. She'd wanted to take Sam out of the league and the team, had wondered if the constant disappointment was worth it, except Sam hadn't wanted to let her teammates down. Little did she know they probably wouldn't have even noticed whether she came or not.

It broke her heart each and every time.

Roarke's brothers had played baseball through school and he'd been spending time with her working on her catching and batting. Her skill and confidence had improved, but game play could be completely different.

Marina held her breath at the pitch, but she needn't have worried. Sam hit a clean hit on the first ball to a gap in the outfield and the home crowd cheered her on as she ran. When she was safe on first base she turned and looked straight at Roarke. She always knew exactly where he was sitting. She smiled and pointed a finger right at him.

Marina laughed at the sheer joy on her face, the silliness of the gesture, the bond this harsh man and her daughter had built. Tears stung at the back of her throat.

"I want to marry you."

Roarke's words were so quiet, so low, they didn't register at first.

"I— What?" she managed.

"I want to marry you."

All at once it felt as if the oxygen had been sucked from the warm morning air. He hadn't looked at her, was still facing forward watching the game, his profile set in harsh lines.

She hadn't imagined it, had she?

"You—you're proposing to me at a kid's softball game?" she breathed.

He looked down at his hands, clasped between his wide-spread thighs. "The kid and I made a deal."

Marina frowned. "A deal? What kind of deal?"

"That if she made it to first base, I'd ask you."

"*What?*"

"The deal part was all her idea."

"Roarke—"

"You're stalling." His gaze lifted to hers then, dark and piercing. "I just need one word, Marina."

Well, she'd give him a word all right. "Why?"

His mouth lifted at one corner. "Not the word I was after."

He'd already asked her if she'd move into his house with him. He'd finished the renovation, but he hadn't put it on the market. As it turned out, Roarke flipped around ten houses a year, but this one he'd kept, made it into a home, a huge, gorgeous home. He'd told her yesterday he was planning to build a batting cage in the large backyard.

She bit her lip. "Roarke, I—I don't want you to feel you have to, you know, because of Sam. If it's for her benefit, for appearances, then—"

"The kid…" He cleared his throat. "She told me she loved me last week. When we were practicing down here on the field."

"Oh."

Wow.

"Yeah." He swallowed. "I figured if she can say it, just like that, I can man-up and do the same."

Oh God.

He looked at her then, direct and laser focused. "I love you, Marina and I've never said that to another woman. Ever. I love you and I love the kid. That's why. That's it. That's all I've got."

She had no time to prepare for the impact of the words, no time to anticipate how they'd sound, how they'd make her feel. She'd been okay never hearing them from him because she didn't need the words. He showed her every day. In every touch, every word, every look.

But God...the words. They roared through her—so simple, so powerful. Maybe she'd needed them after all.

"I—I've already been married, Roarke."

His dark brows shot down over his eyes. "So?"

She'd regret having ever met Stuart if it weren't for Sam. He'd been a mistake, plain and simple. One she'd sworn she'd never repeat.

"So, it didn't work out so great."

"Yeah, thank fuck for that," he forced out.

"Roarke—"

"So, do you have a word now?"

He was all rugged confidence, but Marina saw the hint of uncertainty under it, the air of vulnerability she now knew he only ever let her see.

"Yes," she whispered. There was no other word, no other choice, and in that moment she'd never been more sure of anything in her life.

One eyebrow lifted. The gesture might have seemed casual, even arrogant, but she'd seen his jaw clench. "Yes, you have another word? Or is the word *yes?*"

"The word is...*yes.*"

He let out a heavy breath and reached out his hand to her. She placed her palm against his—warm and rough—sliding her fingers between his until they were laced together. Tight and strong. One.

"I'd kiss you right now," he rasped, his gaze dropping to her mouth. "But I wouldn't want to stop. Later. Okay?"

There was a solemn promise in his words, an explicit vow. She nodded, not trusting her voice.

Roarke turned toward the field. He pointed at

Sam, smiled and gave her a thumbs-up. She shrieked, laughed, jumped up and down.

Marina's chest tightened. She'd never seen Sam so happy. *She'd* never been so happy. She squeezed Roarke's hand, felt him tighten his hold in return. Because they were a family. Her family.

Thank you for reading and I hope you enjoyed BREAK DOWN, the fourth book in my Men Out of Uniform series.

SO...NOW WHAT?

Read my **other books**?

MEN OUT OF UNIFORM SERIES
PIN DOWN
NAIL DOWN
TAKE DOWN
BREAK DOWN

HOT FIREFIGHTER SERIES
PAY UP
PICK UP

STAND-ALONE
PLAY ME
POINT BLANK
PICTURE THIS

Join my **newsletter**?

Join my mailing list for book release news. I will never spam you. Link is on my website - www.kailyhart.com.

Follow me on Facebook?

You'll find me at KailyHartAuthor. I share book and character related stuff here.

Join my closed Facebook Group?

Come **find me** at Kaily's HartThrobs on Facebook. This is a closed group for readers and I share all of my news here *first*.

All of the above? Heck, why not?

KEEP READING FOR A SNEAK PEAK AT THE OTHER BOOKS IN THE MEN OUT OF UNIFORM SERIES....

PIN DOWN
(MEN OUT OF UNIFORM BOOK 1)

For Nash Carmichael, this downtime was meant to be like any other. Pick a random city and settle in for some much needed R&R—of the adult variety. Except Nash didn't count on meeting Lexi. He'd written her off as too young, too blonde and too "cute" for his brand of entertainment…until her smart mouth intrigues the hell out of him.

Alexis "Lexi" Ryan might be outwardly tough and plenty sarcastic, a byproduct of her crappy childhood, but it's pretty much all for show. Fact is, she's got a big-ass problem—one she's kept from everyone, one she hasn't been able to solve on her own. So how then does the hot, gorgeous, "it's just sex" guy manage to zero right in on it? And somehow fix it?

Nash's only permanent place is a storage unit he hasn't checked in over five years and that's just how he likes it. The sex with Lexi is plenty hot and dirty—just how he likes *it*—but it's sweet too, and not just that. Soon he's trying to remember why he vowed never to be pinned down by anything or anyone.

READ THE FIRST SCENE FROM PIN DOWN…

How exactly did I get roped into this again?

Oh, yeah, the guilt card had been played in a major way and she'd been the sucker who'd caved. Also known as "doing a big-ass favor for a friend". Lexi sighed. It really hadn't been so bad and it was for a good cause, right? At least there'd been some decent eye candy to pass the time, although "decent" might be an understatement. All those fit, hard bodies. Close-cropped hair. And muscles, let's not forget the muscles, a whole hell of a lot of them. And, oh man, add to that a uniform and you had a serious case of "wow".

Just when she figured she'd put in enough time to be able to bow out, she saw him. Some guys had the walk, you know? The signature stride that drew the eye with its easy movement, the one that screamed confidence, the one you just knew meant he had to be awesome in bed. Or at least he thought he was. And this guy had it all going on. He had the same ripped, honed body, yet even in a crowded airport filled with returning serviceman—big, hot, hunky guys—he still somehow managed to stand out.

He wore dark, wrinkled cargo pants that rode low on lean hips and a black t-shirt that had seen better days, the seams stretched to the max over a massive chest and thick biceps. The shirt hung a little loose over a hard, flat stomach and God, how she loved that look on a guy.

His hair was dark and short, sticking up in places as if he'd run impatient fingers through it, and he had at least a day's beard growth covering lean cheeks and the hard angles of his jaw. He should have just looked scruffy, he *was* scruffy, yet he exuded a sharp, savage awareness that had the air almost crackling with energy around him. Despite his casual appearance, his every movement screamed "fighter", plain and simple.

He was rough, rugged and God help her, edible. She had an urge to lift up his t-shirt and taste that hard skin, put her mouth to him, lick him until he whimpered. Would a guy like that whimper? Would he even know how? What she wouldn't give to find out. She took a deep breath at the curl of heat low in her abdomen. It had been too long, way too long, if she was drooling over a guy just because he had a spectacular bod. She snorted to herself. He probably had women hanging all over him on a regular basis and she'd never been much for following the crowd.

And just look at him. He was scanning the area as if he'd prefer to be anywhere but here. Now *that* she could relate to.

Lexi dragged her gaze away with an effort to land on the guy next to him. Oh, so not fair. They were of a similar height and build, but where the first guy was dark, this one was light. He was dressed in sand-colored cargoes, a white t-shirt and except for the hard edge in his gaze, he could have been a beach bum—brown sun-streaked hair, blue eyes and tanned. Separately, they were more than drool-worthy. Together, they almost hurt her eyes they were so stunning. And she wasn't the only one to notice.

She watched with more than a little interest when the blond guy dropped his duffel and embraced the woman who stepped up and straight into his arms as if she belonged there. It was a clutching, clinging hold, his arms wrapped completely around her, almost as if they wanted in each other's skin. Her heart slammed against her ribs, her throat went dry and she felt the heat in her cheeks.

Jeez, guys...get a room already.

Lexi swallowed and looked away. It was intimate, too intimate, and that's when reality set in, hard and fast. She didn't have anyone to hold or anyone to hold her and probably never ever like that anyway. As it was, she wasn't even likely to be getting any action anytime soon. Mr. Hot Bod was staring down at the floor, almost as if he couldn't stand to look at them either. As if sensing her eyes on him, his lids lifted and his dark gaze zeroed right in on her.

Chocolate. The color of his eyes made her think of melted chocolate—dark, decadent and so not good for her. In fact, probably outright bad for her. His look was bold and assessing and unapologetic as hell.

Lexi cleared her throat. "Welcome home, soldier."

Groan.

It wasn't what she'd meant to say but at least she hadn't blurted out what she was really thinking. Yeah, that wouldn't have been good, but it still pissed her off because her voice came out a lot huskier than normal. Why? Because he was a hot guy and pushed her buttons? Every single one of them? Please. He probably had a voice like Mickey Mouse.

"Yeah. Why don't you save that for someone who'll appreciate it more?"

Okay, so he had a deep, gravelly voice that pushed all the aforementioned buttons—*hard*—and then some. She couldn't help thinking about what he'd sound like whispering dirty, naughty things in her ear while he did dirty, naughty things to her body. So maybe he was lacking in the size department. Nah. No guy strutted around like he owned the place with nothing under the hood. Besides, the size of those hands and feet pretty much nixed that thought.

His eyes narrowed on her before he turned away and she ground her teeth together. He hadn't given her more than a cursory once-over. Most of the guys coming through the welcome station were happy to be home, eager to be with friends, family and loved ones. Grateful. Not this sorry, surly ass.

"Jeez, someone needs a hug," she muttered.

His head whipped back around. He looked surprised, as if he'd already dismissed her from his mind and wondered who the hell she was. And he didn't strike her as the type of guy who was surprised very often. His eyes didn't move from hers, but somehow she knew he'd seen as much of her as if he'd slid his gaze up and down her body in a detailed inventory.

"Yeah?" he drawled. "You handing out those too?"

Actually, she'd lost count of the number she'd given today. They'd been brief, casual, simple "welcome homes" and none had gotten her stomach twisted in knots at the mere thought of it.

"Here."

He glanced down at the bottle of chilled water she all but shoved at him. The corner of his mouth lifted. "I don't qualify for the hug then?"

He didn't think she would, Lexi could see that. She'd never backed down from a challenge in her life, even if it was idiotic. In fact, that was one of her weaknesses, probably her biggest one. She'd been here for three long hours, handing out water, snacks and hugs, a whole lot of hugs. She needed to get her kicks where she could, right?

"Why not?" she countered.

Lexi stepped to him before she chickened out, reached a hand up to his shoulder and leaned in. The flesh under her hand was warm and firm. Okay, it was more like rock hard and even through the t-shirt she could feel the heat coming off his big body. Before she could pull back, he'd wrapped an arm around the back of her waist and eased her closer to him. She'd meant the hug to be quick and impersonal, just like all the others, except he was too big, too warm and smelled so damn good she'd forgotten the point of it.

He held her loosely and didn't do anything inappropriate, yet all of a sudden Lexi had difficulty breathing. She swallowed at the wash of heat that surged through her, arrowed down between her legs and caused a stinging ache, deep inside. He smelled like a man should—hot, woodsy with a hint of something elusive that just said "guy", and "hot guy" at that. It was a turn on, plain and simple. *He* was a turn on. God, did he realize what a weapon of mass destruction he was? Yeah, he probably did.

She felt the deep breath he pulled into his lungs and frowned. She eased back and he released her immediately.

He stared at her for a second before a frown appeared between his eyes. "Thanks for the bump and grind, but I gotta go."

Lexi felt heat crawl into her cheeks and clenched her hands into fists. It had nothing to do with her reaction to him. *Nothing*. He was just a rude, obnoxious…

"What the hell is your problem?" she hissed.

One of his eyebrows lifted. "My problem?"

"I'm here, voluntarily and on my own free time as a service to welcome you home and you—"

"So? You want a medal for that?"

"So? *So?*" she all but sputtered. "So, the least you could do—"

"Is what? Christ," he sighed and shook his head. "Do-fucking-gooders."

"Asshole," she muttered under her breath.

"Is that the best you can do?" He laughed, *laughed* and Lexi ground her teeth to keep from saying anything else. "Baby, I've been called a hell of a lot worse than that, believe me."

Baby?

"Come home with me."

Lexi's stomach jolted and for a split second she thought *he'd* said the words. And to her.

Wrong on both counts. They both turned to look at the blond guy at the same time. She'd completely forgotten about him and that had to be saying a lot. If the expression on the dark-haired guy's face was anything to go on, he'd forgotten him too.

Maybe she had rocked his world some—just a little—or at the very least provided an unwelcome distraction.

Mr. Hot Bod gave her a last quick look, cleared his throat and turned away from her. "Nah," he said to the blond guy. "You go enjoy yourself."

Lexi could guess exactly how the blond guy was going to do that if the way the woman was clutching his hand was any indication. Some women had all the luck.

"Come on, man—"

"Fuck, Jake, don't we spend enough time together? Look, I plan to hole up somewhere, get some decent sleep on a soft bed, drink some good quality beer and get laid. As often as possible. Don't need a babysitter for that." He glanced at the other woman. "You get in some quality time, okay?"

"You're not fooling me. Anonymous sex isn't all it's cracked up to be."

He choked out a laugh. "Yeah? I deserve some oblivion. We're both long overdue. You get it your way, I'll get it mine."

He glanced back at her, a single hot glance that said he probably knew what she looked like naked and she didn't exactly do it for him, hoisted his duffel more firmly over his shoulder and walked off. No, sauntered. The way he moved couldn't be called mere walking and *dammit* if she still didn't get a tingle just from watching him.

Lexi sighed, her gaze fixed on the way the soft fabric of his pants hugged the hard curves of his ass, when her phone beeped. God, how she'd come to hate the sound. She should have turned the damn thing off. The sense of dread that was never far from the surface rose up and over her like an ominous blanket, even before she took the phone out of her pocket, flipped open the cover and looked at the text. All the warmth, even the sharp heat of annoyance was gone, replaced in an instant with ice—cold and black—in her gut, deep inside her bones.

She flipped the sound off and slid the phone back into the pocket of her jeans. She glanced around, trying to act normal, trying to *be* normal. Everyone was going about their business, living their everyday lives, taking care of everyday, mundane things. It wasn't fair. It just wasn't. She tried to swallow, but the ice had made its way up into her throat. She hated feeling like this, hated feeling helpless, clueless and scared. And yeah, she couldn't help but be a little resentful. How she wished her only problem was some gorgeous jerk who defined a new level of rude and thought he was God's gift to women. *That* she knew how to handle. This other crap? Not so much.

KAILY HART

NAIL DOWN
(MEN OUT OF UNIFORM BOOK 2)

Ward Andrade. Former Navy SEAL. Reluctant hero. Moody loner. Spectacular in the sack. At least, he had been before the only life he'd ever wanted chewed him up and spit him out. Now? Who the hell knew? It's been three years and he's still taking one day at a time.

Quinn Devlin. Old money. Unapologetic optimist. Complete klutz. Self-confessed black sheep. At least, that's how she's felt her entire life, especially by the people who mattered most. Now? Who cares? After years of battling her family, she's finally living life her way, on her own terms.

Bookish and clumsy weren't attributes Ward normally went for in a woman, but for Quinn, he'd make an exception. Quinn didn't usually get the hots for banged up, surly bad boys either, but when Ward looks at her with those dark, tortured eyes of his, she can't do anything else.

Ward is used to pushing people away, but that doesn't work on Quinn. Besides, she makes him laugh. A first. She's everything he never knew he needed and nothing he deserves, but… He could be hers. For good. All he has to do is let her close.

READ THE FIRST SCENE FROM NAIL DOWN…

Quinn threw herself into the front seat of the car before she got more wet then she already was, although at this point, maybe that was impossible. Of course, when she tried to slam the door closed, it caught on her purse—big time.

Damn.

She grimaced as she yanked, felt the resistance as it broke free. Great. That had to have left a mark. She tossed her armful of grocery bags in the direction of the backseat and winced when she remembered what she had in there.

When she finally had the door closed, she let out a deep breath. She'd sat on gum, broken a heel, spilled coffee down the front of her white shirt—the new one, of course—and had lost an earring…somewhere. She'd also probably just smashed every one of the eggs she'd stopped by the store to pick up. Oh and she was drenched, drowned-rat drenched. Because she'd left her umbrella in her classroom. Again.

She smiled. She had not in fact dropped the breakfast taco she somehow still clutched in her hand. It might be a bit soggy, but it was intact. Hopefully. Breakfast might be long gone but if she couldn't eat breakfast for dinner when she felt like it, what was the point of being an adult? Right?

All in all, it hadn't been such a bad day. Of course, she still had to get home.

She flicked the ignition on so she could at least eat without melting in the steamy heat of the car and groaned. There was one of those flyer thingys on the windshield, under the wiper. Out there. In the pouring rain. She couldn't have noticed it before she got in the car, could she?

No. Because that would have been too easy.

She would have left the thing there except it was right in her field of vision. And she had to use the wipers. And…

Holy hot guy, Batman.

Squinting, she leaned forward to get a better look at the flyer. A man. Doing push-ups. Corded with muscle. Staring right at her, his intense dark eyes daring her to do…something. And, God, those eyes. Could they even be real? The dark-blue rim around the lighter iris had to be Photoshopped because they might just be the most beautiful eyes she'd ever seen on a guy.

Quinn thrust the car door open before she lost her nerve. She had to walk around the door to grab the flyer. She already knew her arms were too short to reach it from the protection of the car. Another fail for short girls everywhere.

She wiped the card against her pants leg when she was back in the car. The picture was a close up of the guy's face, part of his shoulder and arm, his fist on the floor. The wet, sweaty look should have grossed her out, but on this guy? No. It was just freakin' hot. He frowned right at her, his lips drawn back in a slight snarl as if he was pushing himself to his limit and had glanced up just as the photo was taken. Annoyance was clear. There might have also been a touch of savage anger. What was so hot about a pissed-off bad boy?

And talk about arm porn. The guy had some serious biceps. Yeah, that was probably Photoshopped as well. No guy looked that good. That hot. That…

Jeez. She must really need to get some. Quinn sighed. Like that was going to happen anytime soon. The thing was? A woman like her? Shortish, curvyish, clumsyish? Yeah, those chances would be slim to none.

"Gus's Boot Camp" was emblazoned across the front of the flyer. It was one of those programs where people signed up in the name of fitness and got tortured at some ungodly hour in the morning right there in a public park, for everyone to see. Who actually did that?

Quinn's fingers flexed around the taco. It's a wonder it hadn't burned a hole in her hand. And what was this anyway? A kind of divine intervention? She could have looked down, but that would have just depressed the hell out of her. She knew what was there. On the upside? Her boobs might have been considered spectacular by some.

Usually she didn't give a flying fig about her appearance, but this guy? With his muscles on muscles and his get-out-of-my-face attitude? He seemed to be saying "what have you done lately"? Or maybe that was "*who* have you done lately"?

And that would be nothing and nobody.

It wouldn't kill her to get healthier, would it? She didn't exactly have an active lifestyle. Doing laps of her classroom didn't count. Did it? Probably not. The park was even on her way to work. Maybe something like this was the answer? Having some big tough guy yelling at her to get in shape or else?

Her phone rang and she jumped because she'd been staring into *his* eyes. And because she knew who it was before she dug the phone out of her bag.

She was a bad daughter—the worst. She was also chicken. She owned that, but she just wasn't in the right frame of mind today, not for the less than subtle hints to try harder to live up to the family standards. Her mother had perfected the conversation to an art form.

Quinn sighed. She was a disappointment to everyone but herself and even then, it had been a near thing. But it didn't matter, not anymore. She wouldn't let it. She'd promised herself. Because what do you know? There were some people out there she wasn't disappointing on a daily basis.

Quinn looked down again at the flyer. *He* was still challenging her, daring her, as if he knew she'd just trash him the first chance she got. So this is the kind of stuff all those super fit beautiful people did? Commit to a program and stick with it? Yeah, yeah, yeah. She knew that, except...sticking with something wasn't exactly her strength. But this, this she just had to show up to and she didn't need to use any complicated equipment. Right? What did she always say? No time like the present. Your future is created by what you do today, not what you will do tomorrow. Delay is the deadliest form of...

Shit.

Quinn punched in the number from the flyer before she could second-guess herself.

"Andrade."

The voice was hard, rough and more than a little annoyed.

"Um... Hi, I wanted to find out more about the boot camp program?"

There was the slightest pause before a muttered, "Yeah?"

"Well..." Actually, most of the information was on the back of the flyer. "I— It seems expensive."

And really, someone should pay *her* to get up at this unheard of hour. To exercise.

"Look, lady, you want to reduce the size of your

ass, this is the best way to do it. It works. Guaranteed."

"Wow." Quinn's eyebrows shot sky high. Jerk. Sexist, insensitive *jerk*. "Business must be really good," she muttered.

"Yeah? What makes you say that?"

"Are you serious? Have you ever heard of customer service? I could have been offended by that ass comment. I'm a potential client, one who has contacted *you* and you're just... Well, you're rude."

"And you're very perceptive."

Quinn frowned, actually held the phone away from her for a second and looked at it as if it could give her a clue as to what this guy was trying to achieve. Was there some new reverse psychology thing about exercise she didn't know about?

"The program works," he bit out. She almost heard the shrug through the phone. "Look, how about I give you a free one-week trial?"

Could there be a hint of apology in his voice? Or was that just wishful thinking on her part?

"Okay, so if I don't like it within the week, I don't have to pay anything?"

"Oh, you'll hate it, but that's the point. But you'll like the results."

"Ah...okay."

"Good. I'll see you in the morning."

"Tomorrow?"

"Why not? Wear something comfortable and breathable. Bring a drink bottle and a towel. Leave your valuables at home."

Quinn frowned. "Towel?"

"Yeah. You're going to sweat if I have anything to do with it."

"Ah…"

"First class is at five and then every hour on the hour until nine."

"*A.M.?*"

"Yep."

Quinn gulped. "I'm—I'm not really a morning person."

"Who is?"

Quinn kept staring at the phone after he'd hung up.

Holy crap. She'd just signed up for…*exercise*. Along with wondering what she'd just done and why, she had a more immediate problem. What the hell was she going to *wear*?

TAKE DOWN
(MEN OUT OF UNIFORM BOOK 3)

Jake Evans has been fighting his ass off for others and their causes for as long as he can remember and he's had enough. He's outgrown the adrenalin rush he used to crave and it's time to settle down, maybe even get a job that doesn't require him to carry a weapon or get shot at. When he gets dumped by the only woman he's ever really needed, the gracious thing to do would be to just bow out. The problem is, Jake's never been the gracious type and he's not used to giving in.

Raine Daniels has been left dangling for years and *she's* finally had enough. Jake was meant to be a one-night stand—quick, easy and forgettable—except she'd somehow ended up his regular 'thing'. Raine's worked hard to reinvent herself and make a new life, and her nightmare past? Finally way, way behind her. So when Jake comes back into town expecting to take up right where he left off—*again*—Raine knows it's time to cut her losses and move on. Regardless of how good the sex is. No matter how much it hurts.

Jake's been turned down by women before—*plenty*—but Raine is the only one who's ever mattered. Too bad it took him so long to figure it out, especially when some jerk from Raine's past starts harassing her. Hard core. So Jake settles in to do what he does best—take down his target—while trying to convince Raine she can have a life and a future. With him.

READ THE FIRST SCENE FROM TAKE DOWN…

Jake glanced across at the redhead who'd been giving him the open invitation with her eyes since he'd walked into the bar. That would be the invitation that said "anything, anytime, anywhere". It might have been a hell of a long time since he'd been looking at anyone but Raine, but he recognized the message, loud and clear.

"You don't want to do that, man," Nash murmured.

"No?" Jake took a deep pull of his beer, his eyes never leaving the woman. "Why's that?"

"What about…"

Jake cleared his throat against the flash of pain that was sharp and unforgiving. "Raine? Yeah, seeing someone else."

Christ, it hurt to even say her name.

Nash frowned. "She told you that?"

He shrugged. "Not in so many words. Doesn't matter. She cut me loose."

"Jeez, Jake, I'm sorry, man."

"Yeah, how fucked up is that?" He took another gulp of his beer and motioned the waitress for another one. "She waited for me. As far as I know. Every fucking time I came home and she was here, waiting for me. And now I'm finally back to stay for good? She dumps me. Just like that." He snapped his fingers in a short, loud crack. "No fucking reason or any I can understand anyway. She's with someone else. I know it."

"And you're just going to give up? Just like that?"

"She doesn't want me anymore. Told me so."

Jake's voice thickened as he twirled the empty bottle in his hand, kept his eyes lowered. "She ah...told me I'd never satisfied her, you know, in bed. Not really. That I was...ah..."

"That's bullshit, Jake."

Yeah, he wished, except he'd been there. Talk about a kick in the nuts. He might not be good at everything, but he'd always been sure he was good at *that*. Man, who was he kidding? He made damn sure he was an expert at everything he set his mind to. And pleasing Raine? He'd been pretty single-minded about that. At least he thought he had.

Jake let out a rough breath. "Fuck, Nash. Raine was it for me, you know? And I never told her, not once, not a single fucking time that I... I just took it for granted she'd always be here, waiting until *I* was good and ready. Yeah...seriously I don't know what the fuck I'm going to do now."

The first time they'd met Raine had been cool, collected and classy. So not his usual type and probably way out of his league, but he'd been drawn to her anyway. He'd flirted. Why the hell not? He'd needed the practice. It'd been a long time since he'd let himself mingle in the normal world. He'd expected a sharp put down, maybe a polite "not in this lifetime", but she'd flirted back. And taken him home.

His expectations hadn't been high. She'd been nervous that first time and he'd known—picking up rough, from-the-wrong-side-of-town guys wasn't her thing—that he'd been an anomaly. And then he'd gotten her under him. He almost gasped at the slay of sensation that sliced through him at the memory of how she'd felt, how she'd taken him, how she'd rocked his world.

And the satisfying sex he'd been hoping for? The simple relief he'd been after? Mind. Fucking. Blown.

From that instant, sex and Raine had been linked for him. Sex *was* Raine and he hadn't had it with anyone else since. He hadn't wanted it with anyone else and if he was honest with himself? He still didn't.

And just where did that leave him? He glanced across the crowded bar. The redhead was still checking him out. Man, before today he probably never would have even noticed her.

Nash leaned forward. "So do what you do best," he drawled.

"Yeah?" Jake choked out a laugh that had nothing to do with humor. "And what's that exactly?"

Because now? What the fuck did he really know anymore?

"You still want her? She put a lot of time into you, man, that's got to count for something. You've got the skills and the patience, the determination. Use it. Fight for her, my man, fight for her."

Fight for her? Jake snorted. Right. And just how the fuck did he do that? Raine was— She'd been—

Son of a bitch.

He needed to face facts. Raine had dumped his ass. So much for his legendary observation skills, his ability to read people. He'd never seen it coming. No one ever did, did they? Of course, it might have helped if he'd been around some.

Jake leaned back in the booth and fought the urge to curl his hands into fists. He'd always considered himself a patient guy—Mr. Fucking Cool all the way—but he'd been stripped raw and didn't know what to do with the churn in his gut or the icy feeling he hadn't been able to shake. Not since the it's-not-working-for-me-anymore speech that came right before the it's-not-you-it's-me bombshell.

He ground his back teeth together and narrowed his eyes on Nash. The guy had barely been able to keep his eyes off Lexi on the dance floor and it was starting to piss him off.

Anyway, all this was rich coming from Nash. "I'm a free guy, Nash. She cut me loose. Maybe commitment free, mindless fucking is exactly what I need right now. It worked for you for years."

"No. It didn't."

"Right." Jake forced out another laugh he didn't feel in the slightest.

"You're wired differently than me," Nash fired back. "You know it as well as I do."

"You don't think I had any game before Raine? It's not like I wasn't getting my rocks off before her and not just with my hand. And just because you've had a girlfriend for all of five minutes, doesn't mean you're entitled to give me fucking relationship advice. I was with Raine for five years. *Five*. I—"

"And I don't think you know shit about why she really dumped you, so what does that tell *you*?"

Jake ran a rough hand through his hair. God, he needed a fucking haircut. Bad.

Nash just continued to look at him, an eyebrow slightly raised. "Well?" Nash pushed.

Jake dipped his head so that he didn't have to meet Nash's eyes.

Nash was right about something. He wasn't one to give up on anything without a fight so why would he start now? Why the hell should he just bow out?

"No. I have no idea why she dumped me." Yeah, nothing added up, except him being a clueless moron.

He sighed, gave the redhead a long, last look. It would have been so easy to get up, go over there and just go with the fucking flow. But no. He just couldn't make himself do it. "I probably couldn't get it up for anyone else anyway, even if I wanted to."

Which he didn't. Because he belonged to Raine. Only to her. And this wasn't over by a long shot.

PAY UP
(HOT FIREFIGHTER BOOK 1)

Neighbor. Friend. *Lover.*

At least that's what Carly Wagner wanted Rio Reyes to be. She'd settled for two out of three for almost a year and it just wasn't enough. Not anymore. When Rio proposes a bet—of the sexual variety—she knows it's out of character and he's not really serious, yet she can't resist. The payoff could mean finally getting her hands on the gorgeous firefighter she's drooled over since she moved in next door.

The timing had never seemed right for him and Carly, but that hadn't stopped Rio from imagining wild and wicked things about her. It had been a joke—*sort of*—but Rio's shocked when she takes him up on the dumbass bet. Now he's in a world of hurt, because regardless of who wins, he might be crossing a line he never thought he would, and jeopardizing a friendship that means more to him than anything.

READ THE FIRST SCENE FROM PAY UP...

"Yes, yes, Rio, yes...oh...*God*, yes..."
Not again.
Carly felt heat flare in her cheeks, not to mention the other parts of her body. It washed over and through her all at once, leaving her weak, her breathing unsteady, and just plain...hot.
What the hell did Rio do to get them to moan and scream and gasp that way? *She'd* never called out like that in the throes of passion or anywhere else for

that matter. She was also pretty sure it wouldn't have been with that sense of utter abandon or lack of regard for who might hear her. And let's face it, she just wasn't that great an actress.

One of the reasons she'd bought her condo in this building was for its construction, *specifically* the interior concrete walls. It should have been impossible, but some freak design with the ventilation system meant…they had to be going at it up against the entry wall that backed directly to hers. Why hadn't that occurred to her? They'd barely made it past his front door before…

Whew.

Carly inhaled quickly at the sharp pull low in her abdomen. She swore she could hear a faint rhythmic thumping and muffled groans too, but it could just as easily be her imagination taking over. It didn't take much to have her picturing Rio's big body and what he was doing with it to get that kind of response. God, he'd be hot and sweaty, his body gleaming with exertion, his dark hair damp and sticking up where urgent hands had been buried in it, maybe holding on to him, urging him on. He'd have his shirt off, but maybe he'd been impatient, unfastening his pants just enough, having thrust them down roughly so he could—

She took a deep, shaky breath. She really, really needed to get a life. Unfortunately, she'd heard the whispers and giggles for a long time about how awesome Rio was in bed. About how built he was…*down there*, and about how he knew his way around a woman's body like few guys did. Hearing the evidence of it for the second time in a week didn't help.

Carly could feel how damp her panties were against the hot, aching flesh between her legs. She couldn't help the clench of her inner muscles when she heard a definite thud and more with the moaning.

They were still going at it?

She'd figured after that crescendo they'd be done. She sighed. Yeah, she'd heard about Rio's stamina as well.

How could she be hot and bothered and jealous as hell all at once? The hot and bothered she wasn't so surprised about. She only had to picture Rio shirtless and she was there. Hell, she only had to imagine his big hands, the sharp line of his jaw, the flash of his smile or his startling blue eyes and that was enough. The shockingly intense jealousy had sneaked up on her over time. And now? It was like acid burning through her veins at the thought of him and what he was doing with another woman, *to* another woman.

So, who did he have over there?

He hadn't dated anyone regularly since the woman he'd been seeing when they'd first met. He never lacked feminine attention though. Being a tall, dark-haired, ripped firefighter didn't hurt him in that department either, but he didn't play the field like he could. Sometimes he went weeks without seeing anyone. Not that she was keeping track or anything. Aw, jeez, who was she kidding? She knew every woman he'd ever gone out with. It was the second time this week with the sound effects and it was getting on her nerves, not to mention her libido. So, all right…she didn't have to stand in the kitchen, close to her front door where the sound seemed to be the loudest. She could have moved and spared herself, because she wasn't sure her heart could stand much more either, but something kept her rooted to the spot.

She closed her eyes and leaned back against the counter. Her body was on fire, her clothing rough against her overheated skin. Even the softness of her washed-to-death t- shirt seemed abrasive against her pebble-hard nipples. She gasped as the muscles between her legs and deep inside where she burned flexed involuntarily. Her panties were soaked.

Dammit.

It was inevitable. She knew, she just knew, before she went to sleep tonight she was going to be making good use of her vibrator, imagining it was Rio pleasuring her, his unforgiving tongue flickering over the swollen bud of her clitoris before his big body thrust in and out of her as he braced *her* up against the wall. She had to give in to it, there was no choice, because if she held out, the need and want and lust became unbearable. Been there, done that. Greg hadn't been able to satisfy that in her either. Despite how pleasant their sex, he couldn't satisfy the craving she had for Rio. He never had. She snorted. Yeah, thinking sex with him was "pleasant" should have given her more than a clue, a long time ago.

God. Rio Reyes. He'd been her sexy neighbor for just over a year, a good friend for almost the same amount of time and her secret crush since the day he'd helped her "de- wedge" her console table from the apartment elevator. An elevator she wasn't supposed to be using for moving in her furniture. He'd laughed at her with his infectious smile and gorgeous dimples and she'd been gone.

She sighed. Crush was such a lame word to describe the reaction she'd had to him at that first meeting and the *yearning* she'd felt ever since. She'd thought at first it'd been mutual. She would have sworn she hadn't imagined that spark when he'd laughed at her futile attempts to move her table, when he'd helped her carry it up to her new place, when he'd shaken her hand and introduced himself when he realized she was his new neighbor. The feel of his rough hand wrapped around hers had almost caused her to swoon at his feet and Carly wasn't the swooning type. The way he'd looked at her that day…it could still cause her to tremble. She'd learned later he was in a long-term relationship and although they'd eventually broken up, he'd never made a move on her, never shown the slightest interest in her that way.

Rio was nice. Just…nice. It might not sound very exciting, but along with being one of the hottest guys she'd ever seen, he was fun, easygoing, thoughtful and incredibly respectful, especially of women. He also watched his language around her and she'd always thought it was sweet. Add to all of that the fact he was one of San Diego's finest, and the combination was unusual and pretty much irresistible.

Damn, damn, damn.

Carly shoved the ice-cream carton she still held in her hands back into the freezer and slammed the door, wincing when it opened slightly again before finally closing. No way. *No way.* She wouldn't be a fucking stereotype, sitting home alone on a Friday night shoveling vanilla-bean ice cream down her throat and fantasizing about something that was completely out of her reach. So, she got dumped by her boyfriend today. Greg had actually dumped her. *So what?* It wasn't even that she was hurt all that much, but the jerk hadn't had the decency to give her an adequate reason. He hadn't even had the decency to do it in person, and she didn't need an audible reminder that she didn't have anyone to have wild monkey sex with. That the guy she *did* want to have sex with was giving it to someone else.

So yeah, she was mad. Good and mad. Because she'd had doubts about Greg for weeks, maybe months, and she should have been the one to end things. Because she'd never actually had *any* sex that would qualify as "wild monkey sex". *Ever.* Instead, she'd let things slide with Greg, thinking perhaps a less than perfect boyfriend was better than being alone. Because then what would she do? Drool and fantasize about Rio, that's what. And what do you know? It'd been less than four hours and she knew she'd been right. *It sucked.*

ABOUT THE AUTHOR

Kaily Hart, a seemingly straight-laced mother of four, left corporate America and a high-powered, lucrative career to be a stay at home mom. Right… That lasted about four weeks, during which time she realized she had a deeply repressed dream—to write. And (gasp) *romance* at that! Who knew? By day, Kaily plays conservative wife and soccer mom, but at night crafts hot and steamy tales of romance and love with gorgeous heroes who wouldn't dream of leaving the toilet seat up. *Ever*. She's smart and sassy, at least in her own mind, and is creating as many happy ever afters as she can, one hot story at a time. Kaily never would have thought she'd be doing this, but now that she is? Well, you couldn't pay her, *ME* enough to do anything else.

Made in the USA
Middletown, DE
14 October 2018